"When did you

"Nineteen years ago."

"Really!" The expressive eyebrows arched high. "You were a baby then."

Linnet sighed and shifted slightly. "After my father disappeared, his sister Fearn traced him here to central Canada. She insisted he discharge his obligation to us."

One corner of his mouth lifted. "Your aunt sounds like a determined lady."

"Determined! A polite term. She found him, all right. He fled in the night again, but not before he promised support. And he did send money every year—North West drafts from Cumberland House here. But the sums grew smaller and smaller until, a few years, ago, they ceased altogether."

"Now here you are to demand your back pay."

Linnet stiffened and her eyes flashed fire. "I am here, sir, to meet my father and to forgive him for abandoning us. And find him I shall!"

"It so happens I seek him also for what he can tell me. Yours is a quest of love; mine, of duty. I suggest we seek him together—full partners in our mutual quest."

His eyes met hers. They were wonderful eyes, too, pouring out from beneath those dancing brows. Her heart sang. This was going to be a splendid adventure!

WINTERSPRING

Sandy Dengler

Serenade/Saga
BOOKS

of the Zondervan Publishing House
Grand Rapids, Michigan

WINTERSPRING
Copyright © 1985 by Sandy Dengler

Serenade/Saga is an imprint of
The Zondervan Publishing House
1415 Lake Drive, S.E.
Grand Rapids, MI 49506

ISBN 0-310-46632-6

Edited by Anne Severance and Nancye Willis
Designed by Kim Koning

Printed in the United States of America

85 86 87 88 89 90 / 10 9 8 7 6 5 4 3 2 1

For Bill,
who is so patient

CHAPTER 1

Detroit, May 12, 1818

My dearest Father,

I hope this brief letter finds you well and prospering. Aunt Fearn has become slightly hard of hearing. Otherwise she is bearing up well under the ravages of age. She seems happy to consider me safely past the age of marriageability. No, she hasn't changed a whit—she's just as strongly opposed to men as ever. If all women were like her, the generations would end right here.

As I wrote before, I have made plans for marriage on several occasions. Circumstances of some sort or other always prevented union. However, I'll not explain all that now. I look forward to telling you about my "near misses" in person.

Yes, I plan to travel north. Frankly, Father, you are the object of my quest. I shall put you under no obligation, I promise, (except perhaps the bond of filial love). I desire simply to meet you, to talk with you after all these many years.

I understand the ice and snow are receding north-ward. I plan to begin the journey shortly. Since the last letter I received from you, dated September, 1815, arrived from Cumberland House, my journey will start there. Perhaps I shall find you before this letter does! God bless you, dear Father, whatever the future may hold.

> *Respectfully, I am*
> *your dutiful daughter, Linnet*

Clear and dark, the flat river coursed beside her. Its water moved too fast to permit any mirrored reflections. Gaunt evergreen trees crowded close against its banks. Here and there along the shore a straight, stiff fir lay tumbled, a fallen soldier in the war between river and forest. The river gurgled victorious-ly as it passed around and through the drowning branches. The waning sun hung suspended on the sharp tips of the treetops. Daylight lasted forever this far north.

The bark canoe, bearing Linnet MacLeod and her few belongings, fought the river just as bravely as did the forest. It surged against the current, driven by the paddles of six powerful men. They sat two abreast on the big freight packs, before and behind Linnet. The frontmost man, the *avant*, stood braced in the bow and dipped his nine-foot-long paddle here and there. The sternmost man stood also and ruddered, guiding the craft with his own long oar. And they were singing lustily, all of them. These voyageurs sang constantly.

Abruptly the dark water turned a ruffled white. She could hear it crash and roar beyond the bend ahead. Linnet gripped the canoe gunwale tightly and braced herself against the flat bottom.

"Wide on this one, lads!" the bowman called out in French.

Linnet's grasp of the language was none too good. She understood only snatches of the alien babble among these canoemen. She should have paid better attention to her studies. But then, it was so many years ago since she last even thought of speaking French.

The canoe's prow bucked upward as they plunged into the rapids. Despite its length the craft lurched and pitched. Though they were going upstream in rough water, their speed was picking up noticeably. The wild whiteness splashed Linnet's bare arm and knuckles.

"Inside!" the bowman called frantically.

The canoe slipped sideways and lunged ahead. Certainly these seasoned voyageurs were in control, and the rapids mild compared with many others. Still, Linnet felt a deep and unsettling fear. At the beginning of this leg of her journey, the men had assured her the midpoint of the canoe provided the smoothest, easiest ride. It pitched least here, they said. She wished they hadn't said that, for it pitched quite a lot, she thought.

The river broadened and smoothed out; the roar faded behind them. The travelers popped out of dark and lowering forest onto a glowing lake just as the last bit of sun dropped below the distant trees. For a few minutes the glassy water swam red. The paddlers took up their song again, some sort of ribald French ditty, no doubt.

Linnet felt a compulsive urge to hurry, to hasten her quest. She had spent far too long at Fort William. What a wild and frightening experience that was! She understood that trading post operators from the hinterlands brought their furs to rendezvous at the fort on Thunder Bay, just as the suppliers brought their trade goods. She knew that all the canoes in Canada

9

would be beached there, so she, too, traveled to Thunder Bay.

She had no furs to trade, no supplies to exchange. Wishing simply to find transportation north to Cumberland House, she had bought passage on the first canoe northbound—this one—and still she had been stuck at Fort William for nearly a month. And all that time, while drunken carousing swirled around her, she had been literally hidden away in a tiny room in a lodging house on the east side of the square. The square. Fort William could hardly be called a fort. It was more a small city of sturdy buildings, numerous shops and stores. The voyageurs had acted reluctant to leave Thunder Bay—Linnet couldn't wait to get out.

The paddler directly behind her leaned forward. "Cumberland House ahead, *ma'amselle*. You have arrived."

She craned her neck to see around the man in front.

Cumberland House was the Northwest's major supply depot, linking Hudson's Bay far to the northeast with the company's western fur posts, and Montreal far to the southeast with the North West Company's far-flung outposts. One would think a place so important would *appear* important—dignified, imposing. Instead, it looked cramped and cluttered.

Tents, log huts, tipis, and wigwams peppered the grassy, sloping lake shore. Between the buildings, such as they were, lay jumbles of firewood, fish-drying racks, and all manner of beached canoes and rafts. Little orange fires flickered, reminding her of a dense cloud of fireflies. Like mother hens surrounded by myriad chicks, two vast, sprawling stockades loomed on the hillcrest above all that clutter.

The voyageurs launched into a song with a quicker cadence. They leaned into their paddles with fresh

10

vigor. Their craft cut across the glossy water to a dock at the shore, directly toward the unyielding pilings. Suddenly its stern swung aside. Its bulging side bumped tenderly against the dock. Linnet was never so happy to see a dock. Always before on her journey thus far (over five weeks of bobbing in these fragile boats!), a hefty voyageur would lift her bodily out and carry her ashore on his shoulder. She never quite got used to being hauled out like one of the packs.

But then she had never exited a canoe onto a dock, either. She stood up cautiously. Her legs complained, incredibly stiff. Strong hands suddenly gripped her arms and swept her upward. She stood erect on solid land. What a delicious feeling! With a cheerful nod and grin, two swarthy paddlers put her carpetbags ashore.

"*Merci*," she smiled. "*Merci beaucoup*." She picked up her bags and walked upslope toward— toward where? Here were two forts. She turned to the *avant*. "Which one is the North West Company facility, please? *Les Canadiennes?*"

"*A gauche, ma'amselle*."

"Thank you. *Merci*." She plodded up the hill. As she approached, a second choice confronted her. The North West facility was actually two forts. The one on the far left was clearly many years old. Its exposed wood sulked gray and weathered in the waning light. The bark flaked away from its stockade pilings. The site to the right was so new it still smelled of fresh sapwood. Undoubtedly the chief factor must live in the spacious new quarters. She angled off toward the new stockade, rehearsing mentally what she would say.

First, she must not call the man a chief factor. Hudson's Bay Company called its officers factors; so far as she knew, North West Company did not. Moreover, there seemed to be a fairly intense rivalry

11

between the two firms. She must not ruffle feathers by using the wrong title. Diplomacy.

Indeed, this matter involved far more than diplomacy. For years, even south in Detroit, Linnet had listened, wide-eyed, to tales of company rivalry as these two giants wrestled for the lion's share of the northern fur trade. Stories of confrontations and arrests, of ambushes and fights, of violence and even death, were too numerous to be merely backwoods fancy. There was danger here if you belonged to the wrong company. She had heard about barrels and barrels of rum or whisky used to bribe Indians into bringing more furs for trade. Bold explorers, half-wild trappers who thought nothing of traversing five hundred miles by dogsled or canoe—Linnet believed it all, for she had seen the North West Company voyageurs.

She paused on the steep path, suddenly caught up in a wave of doubt. Englishmen, Frenchmen, half-breeds, Scotsmen all shared a common element here—a strength stronger than this wilderness. Linnet had spent her life in or near a city, albeit a small one. She was no match for the puniest of these men, or even of their women. This hideous company rivalry between Hudson's Bay men and North Westers might be sparked into flame by any thoughtless word or action on her part. She had deliberately placed herself inside a tinderbox which could ignite any moment; now, too late, she regretted it. She regretted traveling so far. She regretted penetrating so deeply into this wild and alien land. And yet, she could not bear the thought of giving up and turning back. She had a purpose in this journey; she must not let fear bring failure. She took a deep breath, more a shudder than a sigh, and started walking again.

She would tread carefully the line between the two companies. She would, as best she could, avoid getting between the two scuffling giants, lest she be trampled in the fray. Here was the gate of the newer stockade.

Linnet stopped as a tall, lithe man came striding out the gate. He cut quite a picture in billowing white shirt sleeves and a vivid, striped vest. Linnet had never seen a waistcoat quite that—well, quite that loud. She wished it were daylight. Was that striping black or some dark color?

The man stopped cold and stared at her. His eyes traveled from top to toe and up again. She considered his bold gaze an affront.

She manufactured a smile. "I wish to speak to the man in charge. Can you direct me?"

"All sorts of people in charge here, Missy. Take your pick." He half smiled. "I'm in charge of about as much as anyone around here."

His tone of voice put Linnet on her guard. "I was thinking more of a chief officer of some kind. The head man."

"Oh—him. He's not top dog just now, and he's not here." The man stepped in close. "I'll show you around until he gets back." He reached for her bags.

She yanked her bags back and clutched them close. "Thank you, no. I'll wait for him elsewhere." She turned quickly and marched off toward the older of the stockades.

The saucy fellow snickered; no doubt she was walking in the wrong direction. She paused in the great log gate. She put down one bag to slap at a whining mosquito. The mosquito had ample cause to whine over the lean pickings. A million mosquitoes preceding it had drained her dry. With a quiet little scuff her bag disappeared. She wheeled.

The tall fellow grinned. "Like I said, I'll show you around. Call me Gib." He jerked her other bag out of her hand and turned away.

All she could do was follow. "We're walking away from the fort. Are you a North West Company employee?"

"Nope."

"Hudson's Bay Company, then. You know, I really don't have any business with your organization. I'd rather not even . . ."

"I said I'd show you around. It may not look like it, but this here's a regular city. Lots of business opportunities here for you."

"Business opp . . . ?" She wasn't quite sure what he meant, but she didn't like the implication.

They wound down the hill through the tangle of tents, shanties, and round bark wigwams. Everyone who saw her gaped. Was she the only white woman in this forsaken corner of the world? It would seem so. Hers was the only light brown hair, the only blue eyes in the whole settlement. She undoubtedly possessed the only freckles at Cumberland House—seven or eight tiny dots that had survived her childhood. And she was the only person dressed in the clothing of civilization. Her soft cotton dress flowed out—to catch on every bush and grass tuft, it seemed—its skirts flying free from the bust-high waistline. She shouldn't be wearing these sandals in such soggy country, either; they felt even more uncomfortable than the white muslin dress. And her sandal-ties, crisscrossing up her shins, kept coming loose and creeping down. Even her shawl, lovingly crocheted by her Aunt Fearn, was too flimsy for this rough country.

Gib waved toward a log hut. "That's a saloon, more or less. Booze in front, cards in back. The girls work both places. This here's Merry Maizie's place. She's half-breed. Stay away from her tent. She carries a knife. The wigwam there is Half-way Charlie's. You'll like him. He's down at Fort William now, though."

"Look, Mr. . . . ah . . . Gib. I don't . . ."

"And this here's where I'm staying—me and some buddies." Gib stopped beside a large canvas tent. Its walls glowed softly from the light inside. Across the glow swam shadows of men, apparently sitting near a lamp. Gib threw the flap open. "Come on in, and welcome. Have a drink."

Two totally disheveled men in buckskin turned to look at her.

She must think fast! She hesitated. "I prefer to leave my bags outside, please. Just put them down anywhere." She waved a hand aimlessly toward the tent flap.

"Sure." He set the bags down and pushed the flap open wider.

She doubted Gib was as besotted as his two mangy companions, but perhaps his reflexes were slow. She snatched her bags and was off at a run.

Gib shouted. She ran faster. He caught up to her, of course, and quite easily. He grabbed her arm and dragged her to a stop. "Now Missy! That ain't friendly!"

"Neither am I," barked a gruff voice nearby.

Gib and Linnet both spun around to see who owned the voice.

The fellow looked more like a bear than a man. He was nearly as wide as tall. Long gray hair and beard bushed out to frame his pudgy face. He wore the standard buckskin attire of a trapper, but a Scots tam-o'-shanter perched at a jaunty angle on his head. Its cockade was a soft, ripply owl feather. He came striding up and pushed himself roughly between Gib and Linnet.

"If the lady were running toward ye now, Gib, I'd question 'er good sense but I'd let ye be. As it is, y'd best find y'r sport elsewhere."

"Ain't your concern, MacPherson."

15

"'Tis now." The bear kept a beaded knife sheath in the bright sash around his waist. He drew it just far enough to expose the shiny blade.

Sullenly Gib stared at the knife, at the bear, at Linnet. He turned on his heel and stalked back toward his tent.

The bear pushed the blade out of sight in its sheath. "Can't abide a feller who forces himself on a lady." He chuckled. "'Less, of course, the feller's m'self. Ye have business here, lass?"

"With North West Company. But it's nearly dark. I don't suppose anyone's around now."

"Let's go see." He took her two bags, wrapping a single massive paw around both handles at once. "Wooly MacPherson at y'r service." He started uphill. Again she was being led through the random clutter of hovels. She tried not to stare as she looked him over. He must be a man who traveled widely; his buckskins could never get that dirty in one place.

"Mr. MacPherson. My name—"

"Wooly."

"Wooly. My name is Linnet MacLeod. I'm seeking news of my father Innis. Do you know him?"

The bear paused and stepped aside to squint at her in the gray half-light. "Aye, ye could be his daughter, at that. The eyebrows, especially. And the hair." He put two feet of space between himself and her. "It's more than I care to tangle with." He resumed walking. "Pleased to meet ye, though."

Linnet glanced back over her shoulder. "Perhaps we'd best walk faster. That Gib and his friends are coming toward us."

Somehow the lewd Gib looked taller and more dangerous when flanked by his two burly companions. The three of them were fifty feet behind and rapidly closing the distance.

The bear looked back and snorted. "'Tis nowise

dignified to run, lass, but it's surely the better part of valor. Here we go!'' His paw engulfed her wrist as he took off at a wallowing gallop. Linnet tried desperately to keep up, but with every stride he was nearly pulling her off her feet. A sandal thong loosened. Soon she'd be hobbling along with a flapping sandal sole. She was frightened now, and the fear kept growing.

"Hah! Saved! . . . Mr. McLaren, sir!'' the bear called out. "Hold there!''

In the deep gloom a hundred yards ahead, a man in a dark coat walked along a path. He stopped and turned to watch them. Wooly was still breathing comfortably as he came lumbering up to this fellow. Linnet was not used to running headlong for any distance. She took in the cool, dank air in heavy gulps, unable to speak.

The man before her wore loose wool trousers and the heavy wool coat of an English country gentleman—bulky collar and lapels, gaping patch pockets. Though his hair was covered by a seaman's cap, she guessed it was dark, for dark sideboards, two big splotches in the dim light, extended from his temples down the sides of his jaw. He was an inch or two short of six feet and he wore glasses—those little wire-rimmed glasses popularized by Ben Franklin thirty years ago. How could this gentleman save them when they faced demolition by woods-toughened thugs?

Linnet looked back. The three had stopped. They cowered in the gloom, eyeing the stranger cautiously, as a small dog sizes up a larger one.

"This is Linnet MacLeod, sir. Simon McLaren, Lass.''

"Miss MacLeod.'' He doffed his seaman's cap. His hair was indeed as dark as the sideboards.

"Aye, as in Mac-Innis.'' The bear smirked knowingly.

The man's expression changed slightly but Linnet could not read it. Was he bemused, or curious, or . . . ?

The bear rumbled on. "I've not touched 'er, sir." He dropped the bags at Mr. McLaren's feet. "Ye might remember that, should the topic come up. I leave 'er in y'r own capable hands."

"What should I do with her?" Mr. McLaren smiled and raised his hand. "Don't tell me. I think I can work this one out on my own." He tipped his head toward Gib. "I assume you interrupted their plans for her."

The bear displayed nine or ten crooked teeth. "Aye, and my pleasure it was, too. Now having done m' duty I leave you two. I've friends to meet and late already." He nodded toward Linnet. "Lass."

She opened her mouth to speak but the bear lumbered off and dissolved into the darkness. She turned to Mr. McLaren. "Don't you suppose those three are just waiting until there are, ah, fewer of us? I mean . . . ah . . . there's safety in numbers and our number just dwindled."

He shook his head slightly. "They're Bay boys, but they know me." He stared off in the darkness so intently that Linnet followed his gaze.

The three had disappeared. The darkness hung empty. Linnet shivered, but only partly from the night chill.

Suddenly Mr. McLaren snapped out of his brief reverie. "Have you eaten yet, Miss MacLeod?"

"Not recently."

"Neither have I." He scooped her bags up, one-handed. He extended his free arm—an invitation.

She laid her hand on his arm, Spanish-style—an acceptance. She was ravenous, for she'd not eaten since noon. They passed several darkened tents and wigwams, strolled past one log hut and entered another.

Linnet stopped cold in the doorway. Mr. McLaren had to push her the last foot in order to close the door behind him. Nearly a dozen odorous men in wool and buckskin sat at rustic slab tables around the room. Along one wall, at a counter equally rustic, a bartender of some sort dispensed drinks from mysterious jugs and bottles. There was no serving wench, no barmaid. One took one's own mug to the counter for refills, apparently. In the space of a few moments, Linnet heard at least five words that would have mortified Aunt Fearn.

She bit her lower lip. "Ah . . . this seems like something of a sordid establishment. Is there a more respectable tavern or inn?"

He piloted her to a corner table and sat down across from her. "This *is* the respectable place. You should see the other one." He plunked a small gold coin on the table. Rather, it was half a gold coin, neatly cut in two across the middle.

Like a trout rising to the lure, the bartender left his counter and crossed to them, his eye fixed on the coin.

"Dinner," was all Mr. McLaren said.

Apparently it was enough. The bartender left.

Simon McLaren leaned both elbows on the table and laced his fingers together. "Innis MacLeod's daughter, hmmm? Does he know you exist?"

"Of course he knows. What a strange question."

"Not in this country. Most men around here have a few sons and daughters they don't know about. Of course, they're half-breeds. You're purely, unmistakably white."

Linnet tried very hard to arrange her face into a casual expression. She must not appear shocked at his references. After all, she had voluntarily left her aunt's protective shelter. She was out in the wide world now, the real world—a very rough world, she was learning all too quickly.

He was still speaking. "Where do you hail from?"

"Detroit. South."

"Ah, yes. The tropics." His voice rumbled almost in undertone. Its edges were roughened slightly by the vibrating Scots brogue so common up here. And yet, the brogue was not Orkney. It was more English—Scots with a touch of London.

"Tropics? Hardly. Though we don't get as much snow by the lakeshore as they do inland."

"I trust you never spent a winter up here, then. Tropics. You're Yankee. American."

"Yes. My mother's from New York."

"But your father is Scots."

"To the core."

Here came dinner—a deep dish of something brown and lumpy. The bartender plunked the food in front of them without ceremony and skulked off. Linnet probed at this lump and that with her spoon. She glanced at Mr. McLaren. He had paused briefly, eyes closed and head bowed, before he picked up his spoon. The gesture of piety jarred her; it seemed so out of place here. But then everything about this man seemed out of place somehow.

"Up from Detroit. You must have passed through Fort William." He seemed as hungry as she. He ate with cheerful determination, but he was no pig. Without making a show of it, he maintained quite respectable manners.

"I nearly got bogged down at Fort William. Every man in the country seemed to be headed there. Like a flock of pigeons. Leaving was the trick. I was stuck there nearly a month."

He frowned. "I don't remember seeing you. And I'm certain I'd have noticed you."

"You were there, too?" She studied the square

20

Scots face for a moment, then waved her spoon. "Now I remember. At some feast one night, you sat just to the left of what's-his-name—William McGillivray—at the main table in the great hall. Isn't it strange that I would remember your face alone out of so many?"

"And where were *you*? I'd surely remember yours."

She giggled. "Hiding just outside the door. You see, there was that main table with all the Scotsmen looking so dignified. Had I walked in, you would all have stared at me. And then across from your long table all those other tables were stuffed full of wild, boisterous, loud, hard-drinking . . ." She waved the spoon again, at a loss for words. ". . . Frenchmen. That's what they were—Frenchmen. I couldn't imagine entering the room with all that going on, and I the only white woman."

The bemused smirk crinkled up into a full-fledged smile of delight. "Too bad your courage failed you. You would have been the toast of the banquet. And had there been a hundred other white women, you still would have been the toast of the banquet."

Her ears felt hot. She murmured a thank you and paid more attention to her dinner. Either the stew wasn't really too bad or she was even hungrier than she thought. "I finally attended a dinner in the great hall the night before I departed," she continued. "You weren't there as I recall, but most of the rest of the world was. You must have come back here early."

He nodded and swallowed. "I've an appointment here at Cumberland any time now. Besides, I've pretty much outgrown carousing."

Carousing. There was certainly that. Constantly. Ponce de Leon looked in the wrong place for his fountain of youth. Everyone else seems to think it's at Fort William.

He whistled sharply toward the bar and called, "Tea!" then he gave her that bemused half-smile again. "I hope you like tea without sugar. There's not a spoonful of sugar in the whole compound that I can find."

"I . . . yes. That's fine."

"I can tell by your accent you spent your life in Detroit. Did your father live there before coming north?" He popped a chunk of food into his mouth.

"No. It's rather complicated, really." Why was her story coming out before this stranger? She didn't want that. "My father came over on an indenture with Hudson's Bay Company. He was seventeen. He lasted a year of the two-year contract and then . . ."

"Which post?"

"Moose Factory. So he jumped contract and went south with some Crees. He spent a few years in Montreal with the North West Company. Then he went south to New York. He met and married my mother there. I was a year old when he left. By then his sister Fearn had emigrated from Scotland. She traced him to Detroit, bundled up Mother and me, and took off after him. She insisted he meet his obligations to us."

One corner of his mouth lifted. "Your aunt sounds like a determined lady."

"Determined! How polite of you to use such a delicate term. She found him, all right. He fled in the night again, but not before he promised support. And he did send money, every year. But the sums grew smaller and smaller. A few years ago, they ceased altogether."

"Now here you are to demand your back pay."

A flush warmed her cheeks. "I take it back; you're not polite at all. I simply want to see my father." She studied the brown glop in her bowl a moment. She really did not want to bare her soul to this stranger, yet, here it all came. "I was less than three when he left. At first I didn't know the loss. But later, when all my friends had fathers and I had none . . . I think I hated him for years. A man I never knew, and I hated him. But that's all past now." She looked at this man across the table. "I think what I want most now is to meet him and forgive him for abandoning us. Does that sound silly?"

"It sounds noble. I've heard it said that the loftiest goal a person can achieve is to vanquish hatred and foster love."

"What a beautiful way to put it." Linnet wished she were more alert. Her thoughts were a bit befogged by weariness, and this conversation held much promise. 'Several times, the payments he sent were made as North West Company drafts. The latest came from here, from Cumberland House. So here I am."

"The North West Company hasn't been exactly prosperous these last few years. Hudson's Bay and a dozen independents are cutting into the fur trade. Dividing the spoils. Your support probably dired up at your end because it dried up at this end. Is your mother alive yet? You didn't mention her."

"She died of diphtheria the year after he left."

"So your aunt raised you. And a lovely job she did, too. Do you have accommodations for tonight?"

She shook her head; the sudden movement muddled her thoughts a bit. She must be wearier than she had thought. "I'm afraid I hadn't thought that far ahead. Do you know what might be available?"

"Very little."

The bartender appeared with a teapot and two clay mugs. He clunked them down and grumbled, "That all?"

"Would you like something more?" Mr. McLaren looked at her.

Even this simple decision came hard. "No. No, this is fine. Thank you."

From his sash the bartender pulled a hatchet and mallet. He laid the hatchet blade on Mr. McLaren's gold coin. Mr. McLaren held his hand up, a "wait" gesture. He adjusted the coin slightly beneath the blade. Both seemed satisfied. The bartender brought the mallet down hard on the hatchet head *clunk!* Linnet jumped. *Clunk, clunk!* The blade parted the coin and sank into the tabletop. The bartender tossed two copper coins on the table—additional change, apparently—and left with his sliver of the coin.

Mr. McLaren pocketed his remaining three-eights of a gold piece. "The tavern here offers rooms but they have no doors, let alone locks. Just curtained doorways. Women aren't always safe here. I suggest Mugwila's house."

She stared at her murky tea. "I'm almost past caring where the bed is, just so long as I can curl up somewhere. It seems I've been sleeping on cold, rocky ground forever. Is this a private home? Who is Mugwila?"

"A Cree woman. I have no idea how old—somewhere between thirty and a hundred. About as wide as tall, and stronger than Wooly and me put together. She hates men. She'd just love to cut a prowler in two, and every man in the territory knows it. Her house is safer than a castle keep. I'll take you there—it's on my way." There was that bemused half-smile again. "This isn't exactly Detroit, is it?" isn't exactly Detroit, is it."

She laughed. "No. Not exactly." She stood up because he did. She really ought to retie her sandal, but she was too tired to bother. She pulled her shawl around her shoulders, protection more against the mosquitoes than against the cold night air.

Gib and his two companions were entering as Linnet reached the door. All three men were bigger than Simon McLaren, yet they stepped aside for him. They reminded Linnet of the unpleasantness a short time ago, and why she was with this unusual Scotsman now. They made her nervous.

Many times as she and Mr. McLaren walked through the darkness, Linnet glanced behind. She half-expected that striped vest to appear out of the blackness.

He spoke after several minutes of silence. "You needn't worry that they might sneak up on us in the dark."

"Why not?"

"We'll know they're coming. We're downwind."

She giggled. "They are a little ripe—the two companions especially. This Mugwila. How much does she charge for lodging?"

"Depends on her recent income. Offer her the smallest coin in your purse. If she refuses it, try the next larger. She loves to dicker, I hear."

"Does she speak English or French?"

"I don't know. I've never met her."

"Then I'd best ask you. I'm going to need different clothing for this climate—and sturdier shoes. Is there a dressmaker . . . ?"

"Since you mention it, may I suggest wool or buckskin?"

"But isn't that too warm for summer?"

"The fabric is to fend off mosquitoes, not chill. I can't help noticing that you're being eaten alive in that flimsy attire." He laid a warm hand on her shoulder to draw her aside between two wigwams. At his touch, a happy little tickle coursed through her. Curious!

He pointed to a miserable hovel built of stacked

25

poles. The hut was smaller by far than Aunt Fearn's
parlor. "Mugwila's house. Oh. In answer to your
question, go down to the dock tomorrow and talk to
the greengrocer. His wife sews." He stood a moment,
hesitating. "This is very forward of me, and I beg
your indulgence. You haven't mentioned any husband
or beau. Are you affianced? Widowed? Happily
married?"

"None of those. Let's say my, ah, various prospects fell through for one reason or another." She
thought a moment and added, "Nor am I seeking new
prospects now. I'm content in my present state."

"You and the apostle St. Paul. Would that far more
people could say that honestly. Miss MacLeod, it was
my pleasure this evening. God bless your quest." He
turned on his heel and left so quickly she replied with
a fumble-tongued "Good evening" to his departing
back.

The dark crowded in close against her. She drew
her shawl tighter around and knocked timidly at
Mugwila's door. Silence. She knocked more urgently
as the darkness pressed closer.

The door creaked open. In the sallow candlelight
stood a broad-faced woman with long stringy hair.
She squinted at Linnet; her eyes, buried somewhere
deep within pudgy creases. Suddenly she moved aside
and opened the door a bit wider. Linnet stepped
inside. If the outside looked smaller than Aunt
Fearn's parlor, the inside looked smaller than the
closet under the staircase.

Apparently Mugwila spoke neither English nor
French. They dickered by grunting and bobbing
heads. Linnet obtained her lodging for practically
nothing.

On the other hand, the lodgings *were* practically
nothing. Mugwila chased a half-grown puppy off a
pallet at one wall and gestured that the little cur's bed

was now Linnet's. The gray ball of fluff flicked its nubby little sickle-tail and curled up against Mugwila's hip. Without a word, the woman went back to her work. She sat beside the fire in the middle of the room, her legs straight out before her, weaving some sort of basket. The fire flickered and waned, dying slowly of malnutrition. Where did the smoke go? Linnet discerned a black hole in the black roof.

Linnet stretched out on her lumpy pallet, so weary she didn't mind the knots. She wished Simon McLaren had not run off so quickly. She had many more questions for him. And she had not thanked him for his kindness. In fact, she had failed to thank Wooly, also. The men must think her lacking in manners! On the other hand, did they seem anxious to pass her off, to get her out of the way? It seemed so—Wooly especially. And why was she more than he cared to tangle with?

Mugwila's house might be safe from men, but creatures with more than two legs abounded. Linnet heard scurrying here and there. Crickets chirped near her ear—very near. She fell asleep too quickly to learn who else lived in this strange little house.

CHAPTER 2

Cumberland House,
July 22, 1818

My dearest Aunt Fearn,

I have arrived at the beginning of the trail, the jumping-off place. I am well and in good spirits, the only problem being that every inch of me is one massive mosquito bump. I have ordered heavier clothes from a local woman, half Indian and half Scots, named Birdsong Shea. The price is reduced as I shall help her make the garments. Still, it lifts quite a bit of weight from my purse. Mrs. Shea is pleased to have the work, of course. There are few ladies here and none well attired.

Ah, my dear Aunt, I don't know if you would be fascinated or aghast, should you meet these strange people. All are misfits in some way, persons who could not possibly fit into a normal society—all save one, that is. He would fit in comfortably anywhere. And my landlady? She doesn't even fit in here. Yet you and she boast a trait in common—she will have

nothing to do with men. I tried several times to speak
to the man in charge here at the North West
Company, a Colin Wilson. He is either elsewhere or
gone completely. And others stop talking to me the
moment I mention my father's name. I can't even
learn if he is still alive. I will continue diligently in my
efforts. And, in the meantime, continue to sew. I'm
very sorry we parted on such acrimonious terms, and
I hope to make it up to you upon my return. God bless
you.

> *With warmest love, I am*
> *your dutiful niece, Linnet*

She was a charming baby with soft curly hair and
huge brown eyes. She sat in the beaten grass wearing
nothing but a little linen smock. She grabbed the
handkerchief off her head and mashed it to the
ground, cackling with delight. Linnet snatched the
hankie away, shook it open and dropped it over the
baby's head again. Just as joyously, the tot pulled it
off.

"Enough is enough, Butterfly." Linnet picked up
her sewing and went back to work.

The baby wadded the hankie and chewed on it a bit.
She waved it vigorously and chewed some more.
Suddenly bored, she cast it aside, executed a half-roll
to her knees and crawled off across the grass to her
mother. Mrs. Shea put her own sewing aside only long
enough to scoop the child into her lap and present a
breast. The baby settled peacefully against her bo-
som. Birdsong Shea went back to work, unmindful of
the child attached to her.

Linnet would love to enjoy Birdsong Shea as a
next-door neighbor, were it possible. Aunt Fearn, tall
and angular and rather severe of build, would say the
lady was "dumpy." But Aunt Fearn rarely smiled,

and Birdsong Shea's broad, square body constantly bubbled with joy and good will. Her little Scots husband exuded good cheer, too. Linnet did not often meet such consistently happy couples. Would she be able to marry as suitably? She often pondered her future mate, should there be one.

This grassy sward was the perfect place to sit and sew. It sopped up the sun and warmed Linnet's poor stiff muscles. (Would her legs ever forgive her for sitting so long in those canoes?) And from here she and Birdsong Shea could watch the comings and goings a hundred yards below them on the dock.

Out on the twinkling lake a huge freight canoe approached. It sidled up to the dock. Mr. Shea, with his big tump-basket of green groceries, jogged down to meet it. A Hudson's Bay man greeted the stern man. The two men gestured at random toward the cargo. All nodded and the freighters began untying the cargo. The factor walked back up the hill toward the stockades.

Here came a second canoe across the bright water, its V wake tracing perfect lines behind it. It was much smaller than these freight canoes and manned by only four paddlers. The bow and stern men sat at their places. Linnet paused in her sewing to watch it. The paddlers drove it nose-first toward shore. Suddenly it ground to a halt and bobbed sideways, three feet from the bank. The bowman hopped out and stood in the water, bracing the huge curved bow.

This was no freight shipment. As far as Linnet could tell, the canoe carried only a small amount of baggage and supplies. There was one passenger aboard, and he stood out like a fir tree among blueberry bushes. Only four men in Detroit dressed as nattily as this man was dressed—the four wealthiest men in Detroit. His close-fitting trousers disappeared into calf-high riding boots with turned tops. His cutaway coat and beaver hat were a welcome relief from the constant parade of buckskin and blanket capotes around here. Linnet could see even from this distance that he wore a neat silk tie and not simply a cravat. He stood head-and-shoulders above the stocky little Scots canoemen—he had to be six feet tall at least.

With that impressive height and physique, he should possess a handsome face and thick hair. Linnet stretched to see better. He had removed the beaver hat in order to run his fingers through his hair. It was sandy-colored, almost red, and wonderfully wavy. An errant curl dropped onto his forehead; he pushed it back. Now the face was in full view. No disappointment there! Linnet forced her attention back to her sewing.

Mrs. Shea was watching her—and giggling.

Linnet giggled, too. "Quite a sight to see, isn't he? And so perfectly dressed. Unfortunately, such men are always married. They're not even worth considering. They'll lie about their status as easily as they change their socks." Linnet shot the fellow a second glance. "But he is a charmer, even at a hundred yards." She busied herself with a side seam.

"You want one that isn't married, aye? Mrs. Shea nodded toward the dock. *That* one isn't married. I know. Word got here this spring before he did. His wife died last winter in Montreal."

Linnet looked and gaped. "You mean *him*? That's Simon McLaren!"

The man himself was walking down the shore to greet the tall stranger. It was the first Linnet had seen of him since the night she came. He shook hands with Mr. Handsome. They talked a few minutes, neither of them smiling. Together they walked upslope toward the North West Company stockades.

"Aye, Simon McLaren. Ye best be careful marryin'

31

him, though. The rumor claims his wife died by his own hand." Mrs. Shea had obviously learned English from her Orkneyman husband. The thick brogue mixed with her strong Cree accent made her nearly impossible to understand sometimes.

"Someone says he killed his wife? Is that what you're saying?"

"Aye," she nodded.

"Impossible! He's so gentle."

"So's a stud horse, 'til you 'tempt to ride him."

"Do you know who the newcomer is? The tall one?"

She shook her head. "Stranger. Hudson's Bay Company, though."

"Mm. I was hoping it was the chief factor. Colin Wilson."

"Is it Wilson ye need, or will any company officer do?"

"I suppose any officer will do."

"Then talk to Mr. McLaren. He ranks above Wilson, ye know, being a Montreal agent."

"He does?" Of course! Linnet should have known that. He had sat at the head table down at Fort William. Only the officers sat there. He was polished despite his humdrum attire. He knew all about the company. She should have pressed him for information that very night they met. Why hadn't she? She was too tired then to think, that was why. It had taken her two days of rest on Mugwila's puppy's lumpy pallet before she felt half her normal self again.

She thought of the way Gib and his carousing chums had fallen back in fear of Simon McLaren. And what had he said? "They're Bay boys, but they know me." Bay boys. Hudson's Bay Company employees—men from the rival firm. Did they know Simon McLaren personally, or by reputation only? The mystery of the man befuddled her thoughts. Fortunately, putting in a side seam required little mental effort.

Shortly before suppertime, Linnet put on her new dress. She felt frumpy. The sleeves came clear to her wrists as planned. The neckline snugged up against her collarbones. The waistline nearly matched her natural waist, but it all hung a bit loose. Frankly, she was disappointed. On the other hand, this wholesale frumpiness was worth it if only she could stem the flow of blood lost to mosquitoes. And you couldn't fault the warmth. Mrs. Shea seemed pleased, and Linnet praised her work highly, since she couldn't say anything much for the style.

Linnet ate with Mugwila that night. The menu? She decided not to ask, but at least it wasn't the puppy. He lay curled up on her pallet, his usual daytime place.

As the sun sank, the lake glowed bright gold and pink. The forest around its rim turned blacker. Linnet presented her back to the shining water and strolled out across the slope to the stockades. Surely Mr. McLaren and the stranger had finished their business by now. She would talk to Mr. McLaren this very evening. If anyone could point her in the right direction, he could.

The North West Company stockade bustled with men completing their day's duties—Indians, trappers, canoemen, a man with fishing gear. Men in buckskin and men in European dress scurried about. Each one who passed Linnet smiled and greeted her. Perhaps her dress was not as frumpy as she had first believed. A portly little Frenchman directed her—in French— to the second door on the left, inside the gate of the old stockade.

Was this the door, or had Linnet misunderstood? The door stood ajar, so she listened a moment.

She recognized Simon McLaren's rumbling bari-

33

tone. "The man's reputation makes him an easy target. I've heard him accused of deeds occurring simultaneously a hundred miles apart. True, he's a renegade. But I need more than your rumors before I'll accept his guilt."

"I told you this isn't rumor. I can only conclude you're shielding him. I expected as much, you know." The answering voice wasn't as rich and deep as Mr. McLaren's, but it was smoother—a lovely upper-class English accent.

"I suppose you'll conclude whatever you wish. But then, if I did know where he was, I probably wouldn't help you anyway."

Linnet knocked timidly. *Go boldly, Linnet!* She stiffened her back and knocked louder.

The baritone voice invited her in.

As Linnet stepped inside, Simon McLaren's face fell. It was as if she were the last person in the world he wanted to see. The thought wrenched her in a most peculiar way. He stood up from behind his desk. Over by the window, the handsome stranger rose, too.

Linnet pushed a smile onto her face. "I apologize for interrupting, gentlemen. I thought your business would be finished by now. I'll return another time. Oh . . ." She spread her arms and made a complete turn in place. "I took your advice, Mr. McLaren. Loose wool. We completed it this evening."

The corners of Mr. McLaren's mouth turned up, but it wasn't quite a smile. "Very nice, Lass. The mosquitoes will rue this day."

"Oh, I sincerely hope so! Good evening."

The stranger cleared his throat pointedly and glanced at Mr. McLaren.

Mr. McLaren inhaled. "Linnet, this is James Landry of Hudson's Bay Company. He just arrived from London, passing through. Linnet here is also passing through."

The stranger crossed to her and reached for her hand. She offered it and he kissed her knuckles softly. "Delighted, Miss, uh . . ."

"MacLeod." Linnet smiled as fetchingly as she knew how. Why had Mr. McLaren neglected to mention her last name?

The stranger's eyebrows lifted significantly. "Indeed! You wouldn't happen to be related to Innis MacLeod?"

"My father, yes."

Even as she spoke, Simon McLaren was coming around the end of his desk. "You smell an opportunity where none exists, Landry. She has no inkling where he is. It's safest if she's kept entirely clear of the matter."

"Safest for whom? I smell far more than an opportunity here, McLaren. I smell a rat. Here's a young lady you classify as a passer-through, yet you know her well enough to advise her in matters of fashion. And she just by chance happens to be MacLeod's daughter. I fear your claim of honesty suffers a few ragged edges."

"Titus 1:15, Landry. Look it up sometime." Mr. McLaren laid that warm hand on Linnet's shoulder again, turned her around, and headed her for the door. "How about tomorrow morning right after breakfast? We'll have all the time we need then to discuss whatever you please."

"Tomorrow morning, then." Here again was that feeling that he was trying to get rid of her. She stepped outside.

Mr. Landry popped right out the door beside her. "Just a moment, Miss MacLeod. I'd like to talk to you, please."

"Of course, Mr. Landry. If you wish."

"She can't help you," Mr. McLaren insisted. "And

you can do great damage, Landry, much more than you realize. I beseech you to leave her alone."

Gib and his ilk might fear Simon McLaren, but James Landry surely did not. "Thank you for your time today, McLaren. I'll be in touch." He turned to Linnet. "If you're not otherwise engaged this evening, I'd like to invite you to dinner."

"Oh, dear. I'm sorry now that I've eaten. Thank you anyway."

"Then join me for a drink to finish the evening. I understand the brandy hasn't arrived yet from York, but there's a bit of rum lingering about, and tea . . ."

"Tea, please."

"Fine. My preference as well." He led Linnet off toward the great gate. "Do you live here, Miss MacLeod?"

Linnet twisted around to call a "Good night, Mr. McLaren!" in parting. She put her mind to the conversation—and to keeping up with Mr. Landry's long strides. "I live in Detroit."

"Traveling alone?"

"Yes." She left it at that. "As Mr. McLaren told you, I'm passing through. You've traveled much farther. Has your trip gone well so far?"

"An interesting journey. The ocean passage was pleasant most of the time, and the trip upriver from York Factory to Cumberland was better than I anticipated. The company's beginning to use proper boats, rather than canoes, over most of the route. A vast improvement."

Linnet asked some random questions about the boats—York boats, Mr. Landry called them—just to prolong the sound of that smooth voice. They walked as they talked, crossing from stockade to stockade, from company to company before entering the bastions of the Hudson's Bay Company. Mr. Landry spoke briefly to a servant and ushered Linnet into a small parlor of some sort. Two Scotsmen in tams sat beside the huge fireplace. They rose quickly and left. Mr. Landry seated Linnet in one of the fur-upholstered armchairs beside the fire. The heat felt good. He took the other chair, across from her.

Linnet tried to concentrate on what this charming man was saying, but Aunt Fearn kept intruding. Oh, not the violent argument that had ensued when Linnet first disclosed her plans, but her aunt's many discourses on what to expect of a man—and what to refuse him. Linnet was not to let any man under any circumstance touch any part of her body normally covered on a summer day. She might permit a chaste kiss before marriage, but nothing more. After marriage, she could expect him to father a child voluntarily, but she ought not expect him to take responsibility for that child voluntarily. This she knew from her own bitter experience. Aunt Fearn had never specifically described the process of engendering babies. Linnet had a pretty fair notion, though. And she was smart enough to know that any action that drastic began with harmless touching, which was in itself forbidden.

All that was theory. Linnet tried to apply these diffuse laws to this particular man and failed miserably. She could not so much as imagine his kissing her. But oh, she loved to sit here and listen to him talk and watch his face.

The face possessed a boyish quality, an animation. The eyebrows moved about freely on that smooth, high forehead. The mouth not only framed his words, it shaped itself to reflect his thoughts of the moment. His hands spread themselves, pointed, clasped and unclasped, folded themselves to repose in his lap, only to snap into action again. She could not imagine those hands touching her.

The tea arrived. "Shall I?" Mr. Landry smiled.

"Please do."

"Sugar?"

"I was given to understand there is no sugar yet this season."

"That surprises me. Usually the North Westers keep their larder stocked much better than we do. I'm going to assume you can get along without sugar but would rather have it."

She laughed, delighted that he was interested enough to make guesses about her. No man had ever paid her this much pure attention before.

He poured her tea in a china cup—none of this clay mug business. He laced it with sugar and passed it across to her. "When did you last see your father?"

"Nineteen years ago."

"Really!" Those eyebrows arched high. "You were a baby. *Nineteen?*"

"That's why I came here—to find him. And that's why I want to talk to Mr. McLaren tomorrow. He may know where I should look."

"Mm. Any particular reason to believe Mr. McLaren knows how to reach him?"

Linnet shrugged. "He's a high official of the company and knows what's going on. He's had dealings with the Métis, and I learned that my father has been living with the Métis, at least intermittently."

"Any idea what region or area?"

She shook her head. "I was lucky to find out that much. Every time I mention Father's name, whoever I'm talking to stops talking. It's frustrating." She cocked her head. "This whole matter is very mysterious. Obviously I'm ignorant of some key fact which everyone else knows. You're a Bay employee. Yet the very first thing you ask me is whether I'm related to Innis MacLeod. And there are other puzzles, too. Exactly who is my father, anyway, and what is he to the people around here?"

The mouth tightened into a grim white line. "You'll be talking to McLaren tomorrow morning. That means you'll get a carefully laundered North West point of view. Yet I hate to be the one . . ." He licked his lips. "When did your father last communicate with you?"

"Three years ago in September, from Cumberland House here."

"Did he mention his plans?"

"No written communication. Only a small draft of money. I've never received a true letter from him."

"Autumn of 1815. Hm." He balanced his teacup in one hand and rubbed his chin with the other. It was a good firm chin, though not as square as Mr. McLaren's. "Two years ago in June the Métis attacked a small colony of settlers along the Red River south of here. They killed twenty-two, including the governor. The colony was not a Hudson's Bay settlement as such, but we had ties. There was some retaliation against the North Westers but the matter remained muddled until . . ."

"Wait. Why retaliate against North Westers if the Métis were responsible?"

"The Métis are quite thick with the North Westers economically, much less so with the Company. The North Westers depend almost entirely upon the Métis to supply provisions for their canoe brigades, and the Métis derive their primary livelihood from the North Westers. They had little reason to do violence to a farming colony except as a favor to the North Westers—to further the rivalry. But that's beside the point. Last fall two of the survivors of the massacre returned to England. They named names. At last authorities had specifics about the culprits. The British government is strapped for personnel just now and the colonial government doesn't seem too eager to buck the North Westers, so the Company sent me

39

here. I'm to investigate and bring back any guilty parties. They'll stand trial in England."

"I see. Where the star witnesses already are, and far from the North West Company's influence."

"Precisely."

"Your first trip to the New World."

He smiled and nodded. That curl dropped down across his forehead again. He didn't seem to notice it. She did.

The man's presence rattled her thoughts and muddled her brain. She forced her mind back to the business at hand. "I think I see! My father lives and works in close contact with the Métis. He knows them. You believe he can help you find the guilty parties—the culprits—and so you were asking me about him." She tilted her head. "That means we both have the same goal. The same quest. You want to find my father so that he can help you bring the proper Métis parties to justice. I'm seeking him simply to meet him—to know him. We have two quests, but the same objective."

He studied her a brief moment. "Very astute! I'm impressed. Yours is a quest of love, mine of duty, but essentially the same, nonetheless."

She raised her teacup. "Then we'd best toast each other's success. I propose this pact: if either of us finds him, the other will be told."

"I suggest a better arrangement. Let's seek him together. If we work separately, we'll duplicate each other's efforts, at least in part. And obviously at least one of us will be in the wrong place when he's found. If we look for him together, we can help each other. Two heads better than one, and all that."

"I . . . that would . . ." How could she say that his quiet suggestion surpassed her wildest dreams? "I should never have come up here alone. I underestimated the danger. I do need a trustworthy man for protection . . ." she paused as if contemplating the idea for the first time. "But won't I slow you down? Are you certain you want me tagging at your heels?"

"No, I don't want you tagging at my heels. Absolutely not." He grinned suddenly, disarmingly. "I want you right at my side—a full partner in our mutual quest."

Linnet had often wondered what pure, crystalline happiness felt like. She was tasting it now, she could tell. She raised her cup again. "Then let's toast our mutual success."

He tapped her cup with his and met her eye to eye. His were wonderful eyes, too, pouring out from beneath those dancing brows. The brows puckered. "You're aware, I'm sure, of the rivalry between the two companies—you might even call it open hostility."

"It's rather obvious, yes."

"Tomorrow learn what you can from Mr. McLaren. But I suggest you not mention any partnership with a Bay Company employee."

"I understand. I'll learn more if I'm one of them—a North Wester, by virtue of my father. No, I'll admit no connection with the nasty Bay Company."

"Nasty Bay Company." He laughed, a delighted tinkling chuckle. "Nasty indeed! Marvelous. Ah, but it's getting late. The sun disappears so late up here that one loses all track of time. Let me see you safely to your quarters." He stood. "I look forward much more to this enterprise today than I did yesterday, Miss MacLeod."

"I most heartily agree, sir!"

Linnet must very carefully reassess everything Aunt Fearn had ever said about men.

CHAPTER 3

Cumberland House,
July 24, 1818

My Dearest Aunt Fearn,

Upon our parting I promised to write at every opportunity. I wrote only two days ago, but this may be the last opportunity for a while. I leave Cumberland House tomorrow.

I am not alone in seeking my father. A Hudson's Bay Company employee wants to find him also in order to seek his help in some legal matter. This gentleman (and he is a gentleman, I assure you) and I have assayed to work together to our mutual end. A North West Company agent, Simon McLaren, insists on accompanying us. I'm not certain why. He mentioned protecting company interests. He also made vague reference to discussing provisioning for his brigades, for we will be making contact with the Métis.

As I understand it, the Métis are a mixed race of French and Indians who keep to themselves. Some of

them hunt buffalo from horseback, riding up along-
side the beasts and shooting them at close range with
large rifles. The women then sun-dry the buffalo meat
and pound it with grease (also with sand, dog hair and
sometimes berries, according to Mr. McL). The final
glop, called Pemmican, looks, feels and smells like a
shoe sole which has been steeped in bog slime for a
year or so. Mr. McL showed me some. This stuff is
apparently the major source of sustenance for the
North West Company's voyageurs and trappers.

My father has been closely associated with these
Métis, including the buffalo hunters. So in the
morning I sally forth on the second leg of my quest.
We will take two small canoes (the craft are nearly
twenty feet long each, but they are small by local
standards), one of H. Bay Co. and the other N W'ers.
Aunt Fearn, I cannot describe the feeling of intense
excitement building inside me, the high pitch of
anticipation. I'm most happy and most hopeful.

With greetings until the next occasion of writing.

> *I am your dutiful niece,*
> *Linnet*

The mysterious and uncommunicative Mugwila sat
beside her fire with her feet straight out before her.
Several days ago she had put aside her baskets. Now
she stitched on something made of leather. Linnet
admired the woman's tireless industry. Like Aunt
Fearn, Mugwila was never idle a moment.

Linnet carefully rolled her summer-weight muslin
dress into a tight, smooth bundle, then jammed her
hairbrush and light shawl into her bulging carpetbag.
She would leave one of her two bags here at the
company fort. Perhaps she should leave this muslin
dress behind, too—there was hardly room for it—but
what if something happened to her wool dress? She

43

wished she could have found a shoemaker. Ah, well. These sandals would just have to do.

She spoke to Mugwila for the sake of hearing a voice, neglecting the fact the woman did not speak English. "Mr. McLaren asked that I be ready by dawn, and I certainly don't want to keep the expedition waiting on the very first day. I suppose that does it. I think I have everything." Linnet sat momentarily near Mugwila's legs. "I do wish I could have brought along my lace-making pillow. Bobbin lace. Oh, we've woven some splendid lengths, Aunt Fearn and I! And I don't even have a book to read when time hangs heavy. Ah, well . . ."

The puppy stood up, stretched and shook itself, then squirmed up into Linnet's lap. She dug all ten fingers down through the thick gray wool and scratched the puppy's back and chest. What was its breed? Indian dog. The little sickle tail arched over its back. If in adulthood it looked like most dogs around here, the tail would curl into a full tight circle.

Linnet lifted the puppy and pushed it toward its pallet. "You may have your bed back. I must go now. Thank you, Mugwila, for your hospitality. Thank you very much. I've appreciated the safety of this haven. Good-by for now." She started to stand.

Mugwila grunted and raised her hand as if to signal that Linnet should wait.

"I really must be going if I'm to be on the dock at dawn . . ."

Mugwila handed her the leather object she was finishing—and another.

Linnet's mouth dropped open. "Moccasins. But . . ."

Mugwila tapped Linnet's bare toes with a pudgy finger.

"Right now? Of course. But . . ." Linnet untied her sandal thongs. She slipped into a moccasin. Quickly she put on the other. "How did you ever get the size so well?" She patted her foot. "They fit perfectly."

Mugwila pointed to one of Linnet's footprints on the dirt floor.

"How clever. You know, I admire you immensely, Mugwila. I wish I could tell you that somehow." She rubbed her fingers together. "How much do I owe you for these fine shoes? How much?"

Mugwila shook her head and made the Indians' universal "no" motion, palms down. She pointed to the door and waved Linnet away.

"But I can't just take these without . . . I mean, they're just beautiful. And I needed them so. And you put so much work into them . . ."

Ignoring her, Mugwila picked up her basket and began to work. Linnet heard the sound of footsteps outside—impatient footsteps.

Somewhere there existed the right words to say, the gracious phrase, the correct gesture. They hung suspended and Linnet could not find them to pluck them. Impulsively, she stretched forward and kissed that broad, soft brow. "Thank you so much," she said again. She bolted to her feet, grabbed her bag and ran out the door with her sandals in her hand.

James Landry and Simon McLaren, with Wooly MacPherson at his elbow, stood by the nearby wigwam watching her.

She hurried to them. "Gentlemen, and good morning to you."

Mr. McLaren tipped his seaman's cap in that smooth way of his.

Mr. Landry doffed his thick beaver hat. "Good morning, Miss MacLeod. You look radiant."

"And you both look sour. You aren't squabbling already, surely."

Mr. Landry smiled broadly. "A spirit of cooperation shall prevail throughout. Just watch. In fact,

45

we've even agreed upon a promising region in which to begin our search. We are, however, bemoaning the lack of a knowledgeable guide who knows that area thoroughly." He took her bag.

"You mean that in this whole settlement, a major crossroads, no one has ever been where we're going?"

The four of them ambled off downhill toward the docks.

Wooly hooked his fat thumbs into his sash. "Simon's been through there, as have I. But we don't know the lay of the land thoroughly, and the Métis do."

"In other words, we're at a military disadvantage. I see." Linnet grimaced. "It's rather like mounting a campaign offensive, isn't it?"

Mr. McLaren nodded and smiled sadly. "Very much so."

"Ye know who knows that territory?" Wooly wagged a paw. "And there's not a breath of hope she'd ever guide us."

"She?" Linnet frowned.

Mr. Landry stopped dead in his tracks. "You mean there is someone here, after all?"

Wooly leered. "Aye, and Linnet knows 'er."

"Mugwila?" Linnet laughed. "Oh, gentlemen, I doubt she'd enter into your service."

Mr. Landry scowled. "We already have one female with us. And Sacajawea guided Lewis and Clark, didn't she? Where is this woman?"

"My landlady," Linnet explained. "But she despises men. She'd never travel in the same canoe with you, let alone help you."

"Is that so?" Mr. Landry's eyes twinkled. He was absolutely rakish. "I don't mean to boast, but I can almost always persuade a lady to a particular way of thinking. No harm trying, what?" He handed Linnet's bag to Wooly.

Wooly started to say that, in this case, there could indeed be harm in trying—Linnet could tell before he spoke—but he saw Simon's face and closed his mouth. Simon was smirking, not in simple amusement, but in devilish anticipation.

Mr. Landry rubbed his hands together. "This should take only a few minutes. We have the time. You say she knows that region well?"

"Spent years there with her family, aye." Wooly nodded.

Mr. Landry led the way back up the hill.

Mr. McLaren paused beside the wigwam. "We'll wait here for you."

Mr. Landry marched right up to the door and knocked boldly. The door opened. Ever courtly, Mr. Landry swooped that hat from head to breast and bowed. A moment later he disappeared inside. The door closed.

Mr. McLaren grunted. "Already he's gotten farther than I would have guessed."

Wooly spat in the dust. "Good thing the sun's nearly up. He's gonna need lots of light for running."

Linnet studied their faces. "You two are really enjoying this, aren't you? I'm ashamed of you both."

Mr. McLaren's eye were blue-gray. Linnet noticed their steely color for the first time as they locked onto her own. "Mr. Landry is exceedingly reluctant to accept advice. That can be dangerous, even fatal, when we get out in the woods where he has no experience of his own. This may help convince him that our advice has some value. Besides, if he should by some chance succeed, we profit greatly."

"I'm beginning to suspect that every single thing you do has some purpose, hidden or otherwise. Don't you ever just . . ."

The dry vertical poles forming the wall of Mugwila's hut cracked and bowed outward suddenly. They sponged back into place. Something crashed inside. The puppy yapped. The door flew open and Mr. Landry came popping out like a cork from a bottle. Hunched over, protecting his head, his mangled hat in his hand, he came charging toward safety, full tilt. An iron pot sailed out the door right behind him and clunked on the ground. The door was shut before the pot had stopped rolling.

Mr. Landry slowed and stopped near Linnet. He straightened to his normal towering six feet. He tugged his waistcoat down, squared his shoulders. His face was pale beneath the skewed beaver hat. He cleared his throat. "She, ah, demurred."

They started down the hill again toward the dock. Linnet said nothing, for if she so much as opened her mouth she would double up laughing. Mr. Landry spent most of the downhill walk trying to force his tortured hat back into its former shape.

The two canoes lolled at dockside, bobbing on the little windwaves.

Linnet stopped and stared. "What is Gib doing here?"

Mr. Landry frowned. "Gib? Oh. Othniel Gibson, my man in charge. I'm pleased you know him—one less introduction to make. The bowman there is George Ross. Also, Durwyn Sims. Ross, Sims, Miss MacLeod."

"Mister Ross. Mister Sims." Linnet nodded toward them. They didn't seem to be of quite the same stripe as Gib, but they shared his air of disdain. They grunted and nodded toward her. Like most canoemen, both of them wore the standard red flannel shirt and stocking cap. Their baggy wool pants were tucked into shin-high moccasins.

Linnet wiggled her own toes. How had Mugwila

48

made these wonderful moccasins waterproof? Linnet stood in dewy-damp grass, so wet that glistening beads hung from the blades, yet her toes were as dry as if they were resting on the kitchen hearth.

Gib grinned at her, leering. "So nice to see you again, *Miss* MacLeod." He plucked her bag from Wooly's hand and stowed it not in the North West Canoe but with the Bay Company baggage. The vertical black and white stripes on his vest looked much like bars on a jail cell window. Linnet almost smiled at the thought. How apt.

This was the first Linnet had watched Gib in full light. He moved like an animal—cat-quick, powerful, smooth. No doubt he *was* an animal, one of the men Aunt Fearn had so sternly warned Linnet about. You couldn't fault his slim waist and hips, or his bulky shoulders. His high boots and his trim pantlegs both buttoned up the sides. He wore a small felt black hat. It would look like a midshipman's hat were it trimmed with a wide ribbon band, but it had no band at all. If Linnet wanted to learn more about men, she had no doubt he'd be quite willing to teach her. She shuddered in revulsion at the thought. He lashed down Mr. Landry's big bag. The more Linnet watched him, the more uncomfortable she grew. And the more she knew she didn't want Othniel Gibson anywhere near her.

Wooly waved an arm toward a small, stocky man in a billowing red shirt and bright sash. "Our *avant*, André Berelais."

Linnet smiled and dipped her head toward him.

"*Ma'amselle.*" The Frenchman bowed graciously. Linnet reflected for a moment on the profound difference between these canoemen—the extreme courtesy of the French voyageurs and the haughty terseness of the British.

George Ross was already kneeling in the bow of the

Bay canoe when Gib settled in the stern and took up his paddle. Durwyn Sims climbed in, followed by Mr. Landry who stepped into the middle and seated himself with a sinuous grace. Linnet admired the way the man carried himself. Even when ducking Mugwila's pots, he had moved smoothly.

With André the bow and Wooly in the stern, the North West canoe was ready to go also. Mr. McLaren supported Linnet with a firm hand as she stepped from the dock onto the keel line and folded her legs for sitting. One moment he was standing on the dock and the next moment he was seated behind her; and in the transition he had gently pushed the canoe out from the dock to give Wooly paddling room. He certainly knew a thing or two about canoes.

Did he know as much about the ladies, or was he the stuffy old hermit he seemed? He intrigued her. Perhaps it was the hint of danger, of volatile fury, born of Birdsong Shea's chance remark. What sort of woman would this man marry? What had his wife been like?

The craft surged forward. It gashed a smooth V wake through the wind ripples. This canoe was small enough that passengers rode tandem style rather than two abreast. Linnet glanced at her knuckles. She was gripping the gunwales so tightly with both hands that her knuckles had turned white. Why was she always nervous in a canoe? she wondered. She forced herself to relax and folded her hands in her lap.

The Bay canoe was ten feet ahead and just off their bow, cutting its own wake. Gib might be a rounder and a cad, but he, too, knew what to do with a canoe. His body flexed, rippling, with each perfect stroke of his paddle. He twisted suddenly and looked back at them. Catching her eye on him, he smirked and winked. Quickly she turned her head away to check out the other side of the lake. The saucy fellow was certainly sold on himself.

Linnet looked back at Simon McLaren. He perched behind her on three points, with his feet braced against the curving sides and his knees drawn up close to his chest. He had draped his flaccid arms across his knees; his hands dangled. He sat as loose as his clothing, totally at peace. He was gazing into the distance far beyond the end of the lake. His eyes sliced to hers. He smiled fleetingly and slipped back into his study of far-ness.

Behind him, Wooly knelt in the stern. The bear dipped and straightened in the familiar rhythm, his eyes also fixed on infinity. These men were both at home just now, both thoroughly in their element. Linnet must develop the same sort of cozy confidence in canoe travel if she were to enjoy this voyage much at all.

She craned her head to look back toward Cumberland House. The clutter on shore was shrouded in the smoke of a thousand morning fires. Already the looming stockades appeared smaller than lifesize. As the canoes turned into a wooded stream, Cumberland House faded from view.

She was on her way, a-questing.

CHAPTER 4

Along some streamside,
July 30, 1818

Dear Hudson's Bay Company, or Chief Factor, or
To Whom it May Concern,

  This letter is to commend your splendid employee,
James Landry. He is handsome, graceful, agile and
sophisticated, but that in itself does not make an
employee splendid. He is quick to learn under what is
sometimes hostile circumstance. Only half his travel-
ing companions in this present journey are members
of your outstanding organization. The rest are em-
ployees of (ahem!) that rival company which shall
remain nameless. Even so, your noble Mr. Landry
keeps a good humour in the face of needling,
criticism, and occasional impatience. In addition he
has learned all manner of new skills and facts. He
would make an excellent woodsman were he not such
an excellent townsman. But quickness in learning
does not of itself make an employee splendid. He is
unerringly faithful to your company and defends it

from every snide word and allegation. I'm sure that must gratify you, but to me it does not make an employee splendid. No. Rather it is his charm, his graciousness, his easy amiability. He treats ladies with kindness, but he does not set us upon inaccessible pedestals, nor does he hold us at arm's length. He treats us as partners and traveling companions, yet all within the bounds of good manners. Frankly I have harboured some serious misgivings about men up to now.

With enthusiasm unbounded, I am your servant Mr Landry's ardent admirer,

Linnet Heston MacLeod

P.S. Mr. Landry claims he has never married, but I'd like some corroboration on that before I believe him wholeheartedly.

Linnet giggled aloud as she scrawled her imaginary signature across this imaginary letter. Wouldn't it be something to actually send such a letter? Perhaps when this adventure was done, she ought to send a letter of commendation to James's superiors in London. She would, of course, leave out all the personal details. And she would phrase the letter—the correctly phrased letter—during the tedious hours she spent on the floor of that canoe. It would be better than staring at André's back.

She stood up from her kneeling position by the creek. She gathered up the china plates, now sparkling clean. She paused, daydreaming. Here was Mr. Landry in a desolate wilderness, yet he was equipped with the basic accouterments of elegance—china plates, proper silverware, napkins. The surroundings might be crude but dining never was, and dining is the most graceful of the social graces. Marvelous man!

"Ah! Here we go." James materialized beside her and took the heavy dishes out of their hands and packed them carefully away in his bag. She gave him the wad of silverware tucked under her arm. He stuffed it in its corner. "I believe we're ready to go. Did you have enough lunch, Linnet? You didn't eat much."

"Sufficient, thank you." She smiled at him. Little did he know her smile was pure happiness. He was interested enough in her to keep an eye on even such minor points as eating. She must amend her imaginary letter to include his thoughtful attention to details of her well-being.

Wooly made an ursine snort of frustration and flung a burning brand into the stream. He took his pipe out of his mouth and stared at it morosely. "Now that it's time to leave, I finally got it lit."

Mr. McLaren chuckled. "Trade places and relax with your pipe. I need the exercise. I'm sick of just sitting."

"Since ye put it that way." Cheerfully Wooly hopped into the canoe behind Linnet's place. Their canoe was upstream of the Bay craft. That meant the North West canoe would lead this afternoon. Linnet got a sterling idea. She took her place in the canoe backward, with her back to André.

She smiled and shrugged as she sat down. "Here are two handsome faces—much better fare to stare at for hours on end than André's back. Not that André's back isn't absolutely handsome, you understand, but . . ."

Wooly roared with delight. He chattered something in French and André beamed.

Mr. McLaren stepped in and knelt. Quickly he flicked his paddle out. Linnet had always before watched the bowman's maneuvers; now she could see first-hand what the stern man did. The stream swished by this point swiftly, all white-speckled and bumpy. Only in this little cove did the water lie flat and quiet.

The canoe nosed out into the water, headed upstream. The current caught the bow. Behind her, the bowman would be reaching out with his paddle now and drawing it in against the side. Mr. McLaren casually slipped his paddle into the water close against the canoe's bulging flank. Effortlessly he gave it a push and a twist outward. The canoe swung around in a half-circle and they were off, bumping downstream.

Mr. McLaren angled his paddle slightly, dragged it, stroked with it. He was enjoying this interlude immensely; his face said so. Wooly, too, was savoring the moment. He leaned back against the thwart, blissfully creating acrid brown smoke. His bushy eyebrows dropped to a flat line across his brow; his eyes closed.

Linnet didn't have to crane her neck to watch the canoe behind them. It hung off to the side beyond Mr. McLaren's shoulder, not fifteen feet away. There was George Ross in the bow paddling stoically along. There sat Durwyn Sims like some statue with wind-up parts. And there *he* was. He had removed his beaver hat. The sun and breeze together ran their fingers through his hair. That errant curl had dropped forward again. Enchanting.

Ah, but this reversing herself in the canoe may have been a terrible mistake. Gib never took his eyes off her. His flirtation began with winking. He wrinkled his nose. He probably thought the gesture alluring; Linnet considered it revolting.

Could it be that this lout thought she'd changed her position to watch him? She shuddered to think it, but that might very well be the case. She cast a final admiring eye upon James Landry and switched her attentions to this canoe. She would simply avoid looking at Gib or his canoe or his party altogether. That should give him the hint.

But now if she stared too much at these two men, they also might get the wrong idea. What an error this had been! Mr. McLaren glanced at her frequently. Perhaps Gib would notice and think Mr. McLaren was the object of her interest. Then again, possibly James would notice and get the same impression, a very wrong conclusion. What a mess!

Presently they bounced down a noisy little rapid and Gib had to mind his work. They entered a broad and shining flat stretch. Gib started watching her again, catlike. Perhaps she ought to strike up a conversation with Wooly. The Bay canoe was twenty feet behind now.

"When we're canoeing downstream like this, why do we always enter the river facing upstream? Isn't that dangerous?"

Wooly unclenched his teeth to remove his pipe, but Mr. McLaren beat him to it. "To keep steerage— control—the canoe must be going faster than the water under it. That's hard to do when y'r just starting out downstream. Ye have better control starting out upstream. Also, there's a line of turbulence between the fast current out in the stream and these quiet backwaters where we stop. It's safest to cut the turbulence, the eddy line, headed upstream."

She wagged her head. "One would think it a fairly simple matter to paddle a canoe. But it's obviously quite an art. I'm impressed. Tell me, Mr. McLaren. Have you ever tipped one over?"

She might as well have dashed a tub of ice-cold water on him. Instantly the expression of pleasant relaxation vanished from his face. His features grew hard and grim. What had she said?

Wooly started talking quickly. "All of us has dumped one now and then, I aver. For m'self, mushrooms do me in. A mushroom is a bulge of water that wells up—a mountain with slick sides, if ye will. When it subsides, ye don't know it's there. Then *whoop!* it boils up under ye. Here ye are, perched on top of a pile of water a yard high and sliding off one side or t'other. Tis the sliding off what does ye in. And whilst we're mentioning it: should ye ever get dumped, Lass, ye grab the canoe and stay with it. Let us come and fetch ye. Can ye swim?''

"No. I never learned.''

Wooly grunted. "Then I needn't bother telling ye to hang fast to the canoe. Ah, but I don't anticipate much problem along these stretches. The best we can recall, there's only a few hazard spots. We can walk around 'em."

They cruised on in silence. Mr. McLaren's face softened by degrees. He sighed a couple times and relaxed, but that look of carefree pleasure had yet to return. What had it been? Did Linnet open some old wound half-closed? Did he at some time lose something of value through carelessness or poor judgment? That couldn't be it. She could not imagine this man being guilty of either error. And his skill—she enjoyed watching him work. Every movement was easy and deliberate. Yet regardless how effortlessly he moved, he always obtained the desired effect.

Wooly dozed. She looked back at James. Gib winked, grinned with forty or fifty teeth hanging out. Mr. McLaren seemed to be glancing at her now and then, almost protectively. He might smile briefly when their eyes met by chance. What a difference there was between Mr. McLaren's pleasant glances and Gib's leer!

She stretched an arm out over the side and let her fingers trail a few moments in the icy water, until the pain made her draw them back in. "It just now occurred to me that we started this trek going upstream. Suddenly we're paddling downstream. We aren't going back the way we came, are we?''

"No. Different drainage," Mr. McLaren replied. "Remember that last long portage? The one George Ross grunted all the way up? That puts us in different waters."

Wooly puffed a moment, building a thick cloud. "George can grunt if he chooses. These are my kind of portages—seven big men and no dunnage to speak of."

Gib was still watching, still leering.

"I can understand the axes and wedges, but why are we carrying a shovel?"

Wooly was quiet a moment. He licked his lips. "Y'd be surprised how handy the thing is, Lass. Doesn't weigh much, and it's no bother lashed under the thwarts here. Bury things or dig things up, make a flat spot for camp and, if a rainstorm threatens to flood ye out in the middle of the night, ye just trench around y'r bed and stay dry. Handy device, a shovel." He puffed. He puffed again. The pipe made a tired, dry little rattling noise. He extracted it from his teeth and stared into the bowl. "Dead. Care to switch places back?"

"No, this is fine."

"Least I can do is help paddle a little." Wooly picked idly at the cord lashing the third paddle under the thwarts.

The stream roared louder up ahead. Linnet twisted very carefully, keeping her weight in place. The water bounced along much choppier just before it disappeared around a sharp bend. They swung wide of a fallen fir tree. Its tip, still green, scratched along the bulging wale.

Behind Linnet, André blurted "*Sacre!*" He screamed something to the canoe behind them.

Linnet looked at Mr. McLaren and saw pure terror.

His face drained white. Wildly he backpaddled a few strokes, then gave it up and set his paddle deep to rudder.

Wooly scrambled to untie the spare. "Hang on tight, Lass!"

Beyond Mr. McLaren's shoulder, Gib and George were backpaddling frantically, braking their canoe against the sweeping current, headed for shore.

Linnet gripped a gunwale in each hand as the canoe bucked high and wide; a torrent of cold water splashed her from the right. A huge wet rock slammed past her fingers. The roaring thunder clogged her ears and mind.

Mr. McLaren yelled "Draw! Draw!" as he jammed his paddle straight down. Bracing it against the gunwale, he pried out. The canoe slipped aside and bucked again. It tilted. Its nose dipped up and down. Water hit Linnet from the other side. Mr. McLaren's face was pasty white, his lips a thin, hard line. Beads of cold sweat popped out on his forehead. No, it was not all sweat; his glasses were sprayed with water. How could he see?

The canoe creaked beneath her. Suddenly her legs and bottom turned icy wet; water squirted straight up through split seams in the birchbark. The canoe lurched and plunged and wagged amongst piles of howling water. Wooly did no paddling as such. He braced and steadied, dipping the paddle blade up and down. There must be six inches of water in the bottom now, some from the broken seam and some splashed in over the side. Mountainous hillocks of water and rock crashed by on all sides.

André shrieked something above the mindless roar and Mr. McLaren shouted in French. They smashed past a half-submerged log jammed among the rocks. They were falling more than floating, through a terrifying tangle of rocks and spray.

Behind her, André leaned very far out and back; she could see his red shirt at the edge of her vision. He planted his paddle vertically, so deep in the water that one hand was submerged. With a wide sweep, Mr. McLaren switched sides and pried. The bow stopped dead, the stern whipped around. They bobbed sideways into a tiny cove and wallowed to a clumsy stop, facing upstream.

Fifty feet downstream of them the water tumbled away into nothing, disappearing completely. Linnet twisted to look upstream. She could not imagine that a canoe could come safely through that thunderous cascade. Raging water literally fell through the boulders, piled up high behind the rocks, then sucked itself into deep troughs between them. Above the cascade hung a shifting curtain of mist.

She watched Simon McLaren anxiously. The color was slow in returning to his cheeks. The grim fear left his eyes by degrees. He balanced his paddle across the gunwales and clung to a shrub beside his ear. Now that it was all over, his hands were shaking.

Wooly shipped his paddle and wrenched himself around. "I take m' hat off to y'r God, Simon. He knew exactly what ye needed to bring back y'r confidence. If this little sleigh ride didn't do it, nothing will. 'Course, in the process He took twenty years off *my* life. Hoot!" He wagged his head.

André was holding onto a streamside aspen sapling. He turned and said something obviously quite complimentary. Mr. McLaren thanked him and said something with *Dieu* in it. His voice was tight and reedy. Wooly turned around to look Mr. McLaren squarely in the eye. "Aye, y'r right. We're to give our praise directly to God and not to y'rself. That's because God's responsible for the fate of canoes. Ye can't take credit for saving this one and ye can't take the blame for losing that one. Do ye ken my meaning?"

Mr. McLaren stared at Wooly for long, long moments. "I ken," he whispered. A sudden shout from the cliffs above them broke his gaze. He looked up.

High in the rocks, among trees perched on the nearly vertical slope, James Landry peered down. "You made it! By Jove, you got through there! I'm amazed, McLaren, bloody amazed. We were all prepared to pick up the pieces below the falls."

"Drop a rope," Wooly called. "We'll haul 'er straight upslope."

James waved an acknowledgment and scrambled off through the trees.

Simon McLaren took a deep breath and looked briefly at the tumultuous water all around him. His mouth tipped into a sad little smile. His soft and rumbling voice was back to normal now. "Thank you, Wooly."

Thanks for what? It was none of Linnet's business and she would not ask, but the whole episode frightened and confused her. She could think of nothing else, even as she helped guide the canoe up the steep cliffside. The men worked and grunted and Linnet herself was pouring sweat by the time they reached level ground. What great turning point had just occurred? What had happened in Simon's life that he should lose confidence in his skills? They were prodigious. Inexperienced as she was, she recognized his proficiency. Surely he knew how good he was.

And another thing bothered her even more. He was rock-hard, invulnerable, completely self-sufficient. And yet Wooly here had just blessed him. That was obvious. Wooly, the lesser in rank, had bestowed something upon Mr. McLaren that he needed. The more Linnet thought about it, the worse her confusion grew.

They portaged the canoes wide around the falls as

61

Linnet's mind drifted elsewhere. When they established the night's camp half a mile downstream, she hardly noticed the beauty of the spot. They prepared supper and Linnet helped with the cooking, but before she had washed the dishes she had forgotten the menu. This was silly! Why should Simon McLaren's problems—or the solution of them, perhaps—put her in such a daze? Still preoccupied, she walked a hundred feet out into the forest for some privacy, then took her time wandering back toward camp.

"Well, hello at last." One moment she was alone and the next moment Gib was blocking her way. She nearly jumped out of her skin. She took a quick step aside and backed squarely into a tree trunk.

He planted himself in front of her, leaning with one arm on the tree trunk. His nose hovered two feet from her own. "I was beginning to think you'd never come out alone when I could meet you."

"Frankly, I prefer to remain alone."

He grinned and ran his fingertips down her cheek. "That's all right, Honey. The lady's supposed to protest her virtue. It's part of the game. Funny. One minute you don't seem to know anything about the game and the next minute you play it like a pro. Bet you know what comes next, right?"

She would have ducked, but his fingers gripped her chin. She would have screamed, but his mouth came down upon hers. She tucked both lips firmly under her teeth.

His head lifted slightly. "Go ahead, play hard to get. Makes it that much more fun."

She twisted her head suddenly and her skull cracked him on the nose. He jerked back. She would have time for only a few choice words.

"Unless you want Simon McLaren on your neck, you'd best back off now."

62

He rubbed his nose, scowling. "McLaren? What . . ."

"We're friends, in case you haven't noticed. Trouble me at your peril. If you want to step in on his, ah, lady friend, that's your business, I suppose. But I strongly recommend against it."

"Don't give me that. You and he ain't . . ."

"No?" She cocked her head. "With whom did I dine the first night I arrived at Cumberland House? And with whom was I conversing today? You can safely bet I wasn't turned around in the canoe to watch *your* vulgar display." Was she holding her voice steady enough, firm enough? Or could he hear the panic inside?

Did he believe her? She apparently raised enough doubt that he backed off slightly. She slipped out from under his leaning arm and walked smartly off toward camp, her head held high. What a superb bit of playacting this was! She must never leave the company of the others again. Yet, as the only female in the expedition, she was going to have to absent herself at certain times.

Well, now she'd really done it! Gib knew the game well, and he could surely see there were no secret little courtship exchanges between Mr. McLaren and herself. But the lie was told, and she certainly couldn't go back to Gib and admit fibbing. There was nothing to do but march straight to Mr. McLaren and tell him about it. He was a religious man; he valued truth. When he saw that Gib had driven her to lie, perhaps he could curb Gib in some way.

But where was he? Glancing about, she saw that he wasn't here among the others in camp. She walked down along the stream shore. There he was at the canoe, checking the gooey patch where the split seam had been caulked. He stood erect and turned in her direction. Excellent! Not only could she talk to him, she could do it privately. She quickened her step.

"Mr. McLaren?"

He stopped and smiled. "Yes, Miss MacLeod."

He had the habit of wandering about as he talked. She stood directly in front of him to keep him in one place. "I have a problem, and I tried to solve it in the wrong way. Unfortunately, I've involved you in my deception."

"Deception?"

"Gib was, ah, crossing the border of good manners. To put him off, ah, I told him you and I were . . . ah . . . quite good friends. I mean *quite* good friends. After all, he did see us together that first night I arrived at Cumberland House. It seemed . . . I mean, he seems afraid of you. He fears you . . . And . . ."

"I'm flattered that you thought of me. An admirable trait, honesty, but I wouldn't worry."

"Oh, I agree! But don't you see what terrible lengths Gib drove me to, that I should lie? Perhaps you might speak to him or . . . or something. I really don't want his attentions."

He was studying her face. His eyes flicked away a few moments and returned. "Actually, I think you may have hit upon a pretty good solution to your problem right here, with your so-called deception." He paused, the expression in his eyes the only clue to the fact that he was listening intently to something— or someone—just out of sight. "Look only at me; don't look around. He's a couple of rods beyond us on the hill, up in the trees—watching us."

Linnet caught her breath, but kept her eyes glued to Mr. McLaren's face.

"Let's reason this out. We know he's watching us, but I don't think he knows that we know that. So the next step seems to be to demonstrate that your little deception isn't so deceptive after all." He laid his wrists on her shoulders and laced his fingers behind her neck.

"You mean you're going to perpetuate a lie?"

"I can't keep an eye on you constantly, and you said he's a nuisance."

"Yes, but . . ."

"Would you prefer to tell him you're fair game?"

"Of course not! But . . . but . . ." She licked her lips. "How . . . ?"

His face had lost that bemused smirk. He was studying her intently—a very soft, pleasant, gentle gaze. He was drawing her toward himself, moving toward her. So this was the clue he would provide the lecherous, spying Gib.

The last young man with the audacity to kiss Linnet had bunched his lips together into a tight little knot. That must be the way it's done, she thought. Linnet did likewise. But the warm lips that came down on hers weren't bunched up at all. They poured across her mouth. They engulfed her. His fingers massaged the nape of her neck a few moments. They slipped to her shoulders as his arms wrapped around her back and pulled her in tightly against him. She forgot all about knotting up her lips. She relaxed her mouth and her thoughts together and felt herself melt into lilting, languid oneness with him.

In time the pressure of his kiss lessened. He cupped the back of her head in one hand. His lips brushed across her cheek and delivered a final little peck to her earlobe. He murmured, "We'll have to repeat the clue now and then; I doubt that just once will convince Gib fully."

"I . . . ah . . . if you think it's best."

"And we'd better start calling each other by our Christian names, don't you think? Linnet and Si-mon."

"Whatever you say," she purred. Curious. She was still floating.

He gazed into her eyes again. The look of bemusement was back, but without the smirk. He put his hands on her shoulders and twisted her around to his side. They strolled casually up the bank toward camp.

Simon stuffed both hands into his pockets. "Now to complete the picture, we should probably abstain from an open display of affection when we're around the others, since up to this point we've been reserved."

"Reserved. Yes." Her feet were touching the ground again—barely.

In all her weighty discourses about men, Aunt Fearn had never mentioned anything remotely like this.

CHAPTER 5

Who-Knows-Where,
August 9, 1818

Dearest Aunt Fearn,

This being Sunday, we have remained for the day at what is loosely called a trading post. It was built last autumn and apparently will be abandoned next spring. Mr. McLaren says this temporary nature of facilities is common, and Mr. Landry says the Hudson's Bay Company London executives complain bitterly that they cannot keep track of their outposts. I can understand why. Mr. McLaren assures me that most letters sent out of this wilderness eventually find their intended destinations. He was hardly reassuring. Apparently I had best write frequently in hopes that a few of the letters reach you.

I am in good health and good spirits. We visited a Métis camp a few days ago. In theory, Mr. McLaren discussed provisioning. In fact, we sought information about my father. Mr. Landry introduced me to most everyone in the camp—even the children—and

told them all about our quest. This upset Mr.
McLaren for some reason, though I don't know why.
He accused Mr. Landry of using me shamefully for
his own ends, and Mr. Landry defended his actions as
being of help to my quest. I really think Mr. McLaren
is making too much of it. He seems unwilling to admit
that Mr. Landry's motives might be pure or selfless.
This squabbling between the companies causes con-
stant friction that is even making me cross, and I am
not a direct party of it. Only one incident so far has
given us pause. None of us is familiar with the
country. Messrs. McLaren and MacPherson thought
we were on one stream when actually we were on
another altogether, and we took a bumpy ride down a
cascade. But all ended well and we are not near a
Métis settlement. Apparently. We shall make contact
with them before the week is out. I feel we are coming
closer.

> *With great excitement I remain,*
> *Your faithful niece, Linnet*

All these streams looked alike. Dark and glowering
trees lined the banks, ramrod straight. The water
either coursed along flat and glassy, or bounced
across rocky spots of various sizes. The water level
was low now, Wooly had said, because the winter's
snow, which so swelled spring waters, had all melted
by now. Frequently they crossed these laughing riffles
by drawing the emptied canoe along with ropes.
Linnet rather enjoyed wading the riffles, feeling the
rushing water wrap around her ankles and tickle her
toes.

They were on flatwater now, and she sat in her
usual place, mindlessly watching the forest pass by.
One would expect all sorts of animals along the
shores. But for a few dragonflies and small bugs that

strode on the water surface. Linnet saw no animals at all. The sky sulked, thickly overcast. A light drizzle started.

Linnet looked back at Wooly in the stern and Simon just behind her. They were both watching the shore intently, grimly. Wooly's eyes had narrowed. Linnet studied Simon's face. He was stolid, noncommittal. In the bow, André spoke in French.

"*Oui. Peut-être,*" Simon replied. "*Dans combien de temps? Yes,* he was saying, *perhaps. How soon?*"

André rattled off a reply too muddled for Linnet to understand. These voyageurs tended to mush whole sentences together into one long polysyllabic word.

Simon reached forward to the pack lashed to the middle thwart between Linnet and himself. He untied one end of the bulky parcel and rummaged a moment. He dragged out a pistol, stuffed it in his belt and dug back into the parcel. Here was another pistol. "André?"

André paused in his paddling and reached back. Simon handed the pistol to Linnet. She nearly dropped it; she would not have guessed a thing so small would weigh so much. André plucked it from her hands and twisted back to paddling position.

Simon secured the bundle and untied Wooly's squirrel gun from its berth beneath the thwarts. Carefully he propped it behind himself where Wooly could grab it in a hurry.

Linnet scowled. "I thought we were meeting Métis."

"We are." Simon was scanning the shoreline again.

"I thought they were our allies. You don't expect trouble, surely."

"It's always wise to be prepared. Trouble comes in many forms."

"Yes, but . . ." She stopped. He didn't seem to be listening. She kept her weight on the keel line and craned upward to see past Wooly. There in the Hudson Bay canoe, James had tucked a pistol in his belt as well. And Gib's long rifle poked out in front of his knees.

"There." Simon's voice dropped to a hush. He pointed toward shore, leaning carefully out around Wooly and signaling something with arm outstretched.

Gib plunged his paddle down along his canoe's flank and pried out. The Bay canoe swung shoreward.

Wooly nosed his canoe into a tangle of weeds at shore. André hopped out to steady the bow and waited to give Linnet a hand. She worked her way forward down the center line, then stepped nimbly ashore. She was getting pretty good at this maneuver.

No one spoke. Here came Wooly ashore with his long rifle. James and his men joined them; all were armed. This bristling of weapons unnerved Linnet a little. It was wise to be prepared, but this looked like war. The men's tense demeanor made her nervous, too. What sort of trouble did they expect? And why did this particular bit of streambank differ from any other place? What had Simon seen "there" that had caused them to stop?

Wooly and Gib dropped to a squatting position and stared at the ground. Wooly straightened and pointed off through the woods. Gib nodded and made some other sweeping gesture. The tension grew. These men were careful to keep complete silence, so she would not ask now. Wooly led off, with Gib at his elbow. James tagged right behind them.

Out of habit Linnet stepped ahead of Simon. His warm hand gripped her arm and dragged her around behind him. She followed obediently. She wanted to keep her heart light—anticipating the moment she would meet her father—but she could not. The men's determination, just a breath short of fear, bred fear in

70

her. And yet, as she followed Simon's broad back, the fear dissipated. Whatever misgivings these men had for the immediate future, Linnet wasn't worried. That strong safe presence comforted her.

Up ahead, Gib and Wooly stopped. The train behind them halted. Wooly caught Simon's eye and flashed some signal. Simon nodded. George and Durwyn joined Gib and together the three moved off to the right through the trees. The striped vest disappeared. Wooly and André dissolved silently into the gloom to the left.

"What's happening?" Linnet whispered. "What did you see?"

"We were watching for a place where the women come down for water–a trail between this temporary camp and their main water supply."

"But there's nothing—no sign . . ."

He smiled briefly, almost a grimace. "Not much sign, true. It seems to be a very small encampment." He turned and nodded to James. James drew his pistol and cradled it in his hand.

Simon led now and James fell in close behind Linnet. The forest canopy not only shut out the light, it collected the drizzle into large, noisy drops. They *blipped* all around. Linnet's feet stayed on solid ground. But just to her right the ground sloped sharply down to a slimy green swamp. Pale green duckweed grew so thickly that the water surface looked stiff enough to stand on. Parts of fallen tree skeletons protruded from the water, all covered with green moss and algae. The swamp chilled the air, made it heavy and dank. A hundred mosquitoes materialized around Linnet's face.

Simon stopped. He murmured. "It seems that no one's home. Watch the woods, Landry." He moved forward, out into a wet little clearing. The forest was eating up this clearing. Second-growth evergreens of some sort crowded its margins so densely that it was a mere hole in a thick green wall. The grassy sward was studded with baby trees in a variety of sizes. The grass ought to be standing knee-high. It ought to be bejeweled with all sorts of lovely summer flowers. But the clearing had been trampled flat and closely grazed. Linnet noticed horse leavings here and there. The local forest Indians did not use horses. Métis used horses. A few temporary brush shelters crowded against the wall on the far side. The *blips* were gone; the misty drizzle sifted down, unhampered. Linnet pressed close to Simon, protecting herself from the ominous silence.

James stepped in beside her. "Abandoned." He tucked his pistol back into his belt. "So where might they have gone from here, McLaren?"

"They're here." Simon's eyes darted all around.

"You're saying they heard us and fled? I thought we did a pretty good job of approaching silently." James was looking all around, too, but he did not seem so worried.

Shadows flitted among the trees beyond the clearing. Were the shadows "them" or were they "us"? Linnet watched James, fascinated. He stood boldly, apparently unmindful of any danger, as if he had not even seen those shadows. Bravery was a sterling virtue in a man, observed Linnet.

"You say they're still around?" James squinted through the drizzle. "Hallo!" he shouted to the stoic trees. "Hallo the camp! Let's talk!" He repeated the invitation in elegant Parisian French.

"I doubt they're going to come running," Simon rumbled. "They . . ."

James snatched Linnet's hand and led her forward. They strode together out into the tree-choked little meadow.

"No! Wait!" Simon grabbed for Linnet's other

arm, but she jerked it away and pressed it against herself. She wanted to go with James. Throughout this trip it seemed as if Simon had been trying to keep her from her quest—blocking her efforts, raising obstacles. Now here he was trying physically to prevent her from doing what she had come all these many miles to do. James understood her; he shared her quest.

"We're seeking Innis MacLeod," James called. "This is his daughter Linnet." James made a slow half-turn, addressing the forest. He translated into French. The silence hung as thick as the drizzle. Linnet felt a twinge of misgiving. They were in the middle of the clearing now. James stopped.

He glanced at her. "Any way to confirm your identity—some greeting, some birthmark?"

Linnet raised her voice. "Father? Papa? You know what Aunt Fearn thinks of men, so she does *not* send greetings. She's as tall and thin as ever." Linnet listened for some sound, any sound. "The scar on Aunt Fearn's right leg never did disappear. It's still there, right below her knee."

"Very good!" James purred. His compliment pleased her immensely.

A dark and looming presence hovered behind Linnet. She wheeled. Simon stood with his back close to her, watching in all directions. She felt closed in and pressed upon, with Simon on one side and James on the other and the heavy, misting rain filling the air all around.

From somewhere in the lowering forest a man shouted. Two guns blasted almost simultaneously. Simon yelled, "Down!" and threw Linnet into the wet grass. Without thinking, she wrapped her arms over her head.

James, too, was down, sprawling on his stomach beside her. "Where? Who?"

Simon's gun exploded near Linnet's ear. She yelped, startled. The sound of running feet skittered in the clearing—several men and at least one horse. In the forest another gun went off. Simon struggled by her elbow. He grunted and rolled against her. Two hands grabbed her arms and in one great swoop yanked her to her feet. Surely it was James—thinking always of her safety and abandoning his own interests.

She looked into the face and screamed. The face of the man who gripped her arms was ruddy, his loose hair black. His eyes crackled like anthracite. He gripped her wrist so tightly she couldn't move her fingers. He wheeled and ran, dragging Linnet toward the woods. She stumbled and staggered in the stubby grass.

Linnet glanced behind. Flat on his back Simon thrashed, locked in a struggle with some stranger in a baggy white shirt. James was trying to roll aside. Suddenly the fellow in the white shirt lifted straight into the air. His bright red leggings flying, he sailed over Simon's head and crashed down on top of James!

Linnet was jerked off her feet. She floundered. The iron-strong hands dragged her back up. And now a second stranger was helping pull her along. A third Métis joined them. All three wore baggy shirts, red leggings and elaborate sashes. The perilous forest closed in around her, cutting her off from the clearing with its gray light. She tried to dig in her heels in resistance, but her moccasin soles skidded along the slimy ground. Her knees buckled and she flopped limply to the wet forest floor.

A black shadow flew past above her head; the two men yanked on her arms so violently that they were nearly pulled from their sockets. Instantly she was free. She rolled to her feet but they slid out from under her. She half tumbled, half slipped down the

74

slope toward that swamp. A fallen tree stopped her just short of the standing water.

Up on solid ground, Simon grappled in the midst of those three. Their legs braced wide, Simon's boots slipped in the wet duff just as badly as did the Métis moccasins. One fellow fell backward. He climbed to his feet, swaying, and lurched forward to join the fight again. Simon's arms exploded up and out. A second fellow came toppling down the slimy bank; he zipped past Linnet and splashed headfirst into the wan green skiff of duckweed. He thrashed, his upper half underwater and his red leggings flailing on the steep bank.

Simon struggled mightily, sandwiched between shirts and sashes. One of the remaining two staggered aside. Here came Wooly charging through the trees! With a howl, he slammed into the fellow apart, and the two went sprawling.

Linnet clawed and scrambled for solid ground. Grabbing a woody little bush, she pulled herself uphill. Simon's adversary fell. He swayed on his knees a moment, then clambered to his feet. He wheeled and nearly fell again in his haste to get away. He ran, not toward the stream nor toward the clearing, but off to some other hidden bit of forest. Simon turned to look at the fellow down there in the water. Linnet looked, too, and was surprised how far up the bank she had come. Wide-eyed, the fellow had wrenched himself around to standing, knee-deep in duckweed. He stared at Simon only a moment. With duckweed clinging to his soppy shirt and hair, he waded out across the fen, splashing like a moose. Linnet watched him go and then renewed her fight with gravity.

Wooly went "Oof!" and rolled aside. His foe slipped away through the trees before either Wooly or Simon could stop him.

Simon took a deep breath. He came down the hill toward her. Bracing his boots in the duff, he reached out to her. She stretched her hand toward his. He grasped her wrist and, with a fluid display of raw power, hauled her straight up the steep bankside. She swayed a moment, overawed by his sheer strength.

Wooly whooped. "Ain't had so much fun in years! Just like the old days, aye, Simon?"

"Just like the old days." Simon smiled—a sad smile. His steel eyes turned to Linnet. "Did they hurt you at all?"

"No, but my shoulder joints will complain mightily, I'm sure. They got quite a jerk. Didn't you stop to think, before you came flying into those men that there were three against one?"

Wooly snorted. "Simon can handle odds like those with no trouble. I just added myself in for the practice." He turned and jogged off toward the clearing.

Simon seemed impatient as well. He wrapped an arm around her shoulders and moved her quickly through the trees. "Could any of those three have been your father? I didn't really get a good look at them, except for that fellow in the slough."

"No." She was running out of breath from walking so rapidly. "I'm sure."

As she stepped from gloom into gray, Wooly came lumbering back across the clearing toward them with that loose, clumsy waddle. He grimaced. "We lost Sims altogether and Ross is none too good."

Linnet gasped. "Lost? You mean . . . ?"

"*Allo!*" André appeared at the far end of the clearing. He carried a huge blanket-wrapped bundle.

"*Regardez!*" Tenderly he set his bundle down in the crushed grass. He lifted one of the blanket corners away from the top of the bulky pile.

It was an old woman, emaciated, quivery, feeble.

76

She sat quietly, staring at the ground before her. Her body was utterly wasted. The skin hung loose around her eyes and jowls. Her hands were warped, all spoiled by arthritic knots and twists. She wore rags; her gray hair, long neglected, hung in soiled strings. And yet there was an elegance about her, a lofty dignity.

Simon knelt close beside the woman and gently laid one hand along the side of her head. The other hand wrapped around her gnarled fingers. In French he asked André if the lady (he called her a gentlelady) had said anything. She had not. Simon asked where André had found her, but Linnet could not translate the reply. Apparently the woman had been alone in the woods.

Linnet plopped down heavily in the wet grass beside Simon. "This is just terrible. We chased the Métis away and they abandoned her. What will happen to her now? If only . . ."

Simon shook his head. "They left her long before we got here. She's been out there alone three or four days." His fingertips brushed her cheek and settled on her neck, groping for the pulse at her throat.

"You mean . . . left her to die?"

James dropped down beside Linnet. "That's barbaric. But then, I suppose if one doesn't find barbarism in this wilderness, where is it to be found?"

Simon rocked back on his heels and folded his arms across his knees. He seemed completely comfortable tied in that tight knot. "She's been ill for some time. Fever line across her lips there. She wasn't abandoned in the sense of being left behind involuntarily. I suggest she just got up one morning and walked off into the woods. By common understanding, no one went looking for her."

The whole idea numbed Linnet. "Suicide in a way.

And one less mouth to feed." She shuddered. "How convenient."

"A matter of necessity, not convenience. Starvation is a constant neighbor in this country."

"But . . . but . . ." Linnet sputtered. "She's so dignified. So . . ."

"Dignified. *Plein de dignité. Oui!*" Simon smiled and switched into his rumbling, crooning French. He seemed at first to be talking to André, but Linnet realized shortly he was speaking to the woman. He was talking about foxes for some reason—*le renard*. He said something about death—*la mort*—and near-death, *à deux doigts de la mort*.

Beside Linnet, James was getting restless. He shifted, sighed, stared at the trees. He picked up a broken buttercup and mindlessly plucked its bruised petals, one by one.

The woman turned her dull black eyes to Simon. "*Non*," she whispered. "*Non*."

"*Bien. Trés bien.*" Simon took both her hands in his. He twisted to see beyond Linnet's head. "Wooly? How about bringing that wineskin in our canoe." His lips pressed together a moment. "And the shovel." He glanced at James. "Is your pistol spent?"

"No. You were dumping people on top of me. I didn't get a chance to fire one off."

"Take his gun along with you, Wooly. Just in case."

James passed his pistol up over his shoulder without looking. "So what's the amended plan, McLaren? Any ideas?"

"No doubt you've done some fox hunting. Know much about foxes?"

"Cunning. Crafty. Seem to enjoy putting one over on you. Tend to stay within a well-defined territory which the fox knows intimately. When you stop to think about it, the hound and the hunter work at a distinct disadvantage."

"Exactly so." Simon nodded. "Our quarry is a fox and we are at the disadvantage."

"You think he's in this area and he's not going to leave it?" James smiled suddenly. "Ah! But now we have *her*." He waved toward the old woman. "She knows where the fox's lair is."

"And you suppose she'd tell you?"

"Her people abandoned her. She owes them nothing. A little fast talking should do wonders for our cause."

Simon chuckled, mirthless. "Mugwila will marry you before this lady will tell you anything."

"Then what use is she?"

Simon stared at James a moment. Abruptly he stood up. "Use? None at all, Landry." His voice dropped to a barely audible rumble. "No use at all."

"What are we going to do for her?" Linnet climbed to her feet. Her shoulders were getting stiff. "We surely won't leave her behind."

"No. We'll find her a comfortable place, probably downstream at that post, or possibly north to the English River."

"Oh splendid!" James snapped. "An invalid to care for. Just what we need. How fortunate I am that the old crone's too weak to throw pots." He strode off across the clearing.

Linnet trotted to him and fell in beside. They strolled across the beaten grass as if the sun were shining. "I'm very proud of you, you know. Mugwila was hardly a lady, yet you behaved yourself flawlessly as a gentleman. And now you have the good grace to joke about what must have been a painful embarrassment. Anyway . . . ah . . . I wanted you to know. . . ah. . . that your fine attitude did not escape my notice."

"Why thank you." He stopped and studied her face. "Since we seem to be exchanging accolades, may I commend your own attitude. At the very outset of this—this exercise in futility—I said I looked forward to our partnership." He wrapped a long arm around her waist and started walking again. "I couldn't have asked for a better partner. You are eager to help, as when you shouted out those secrets about your aunt. You never whine or complain, regardless how uncomfortable the circumstance. You do more than your share of the work—mundane tasks, too, such as cooking and dishes. Thank God you do the cooking. When Wooly gets at the soup it tastes as if he stirred it with his moccasin."

The forest closed behind them. Once they were part of a shattered entourage. Now they were the only two people in the world—Adam and Eve in a cold, wet Eden.

She giggled. "He only cooked that once. And there's not much you can do with cattail roots and muskrat meat."

"Weeds and vermin." James shuddered. "I so look forward to a properly roasted leg of mutton with mint jelly and a plump Yorkshire pudding."

"Boiled corned beef with cabbage and potatoes."

"And everything smothered in onions." His arm hugged her in close, affectionately. "A lady after my own heart."

Years ago she and her girlhood schoolmates spent hours dreaming about handsome beaux, about tall and attractive men, about knights in shining armor. Their concepts of masculine beauty varied a little from girl to girl, but they had all agreed that there existed no such thing as a perfectly handsome man. *Oh, we were wrong, my old school chums! A perfectly handsome man indeed exists and he walks beside me at this very moment. Simon might be solid, even say compassion-*

*ate, but he was certainly not perfectly handsome. She
frowned to herself. Now why should Simon pop into
her thoughts just now?*

"Actually that's much closer to the mark than I
realized at the time." Lady after my own heart.'
You're a lovely woman, Linnet."

She mumbled a thank you, but it seemed inade-
quate. His words sang in her ears. The trees pressed
closer, more intimately. She tipped her face upward.
She stretched as tall as possible without going to
tiptoe. Losing her balance on tiptoe, possible toppling, was hardly romantic.

Certain things require no prior experience, and
sensing when a man is going to kiss you is one of
them. She put away distant and unimportant things,
like their present difficulties and the dripping rain and
the gloom. How actively does the lady participate in a
moment like this? She didn't know. She watched his
eyes soften.

His kiss began soft and gentle. It pressed more
urgently. Theoretically a kiss is a kiss. Yet this kiss
was completely unlike Simon's. This kiss made ardent
promises. They frightened her.

James Landry was a gentleman and her partner.
Surely she could trust James. His kiss became more
insistent, making more promises—frightening, exhilarating promises.

She broke away from him. Like a panicked doe she
ran through the dripping forest—back to Simon and
gray light and misting rain.

CHAPTER 6

At a Métis camp,
August 14, 1818

Dear Aunt Fearn,

Your dutiful niece is most befuddled and discouraged. For one thing, for years I thought I knew my own heart. Suddenly I am uncertain. There is a gentleman who deserves every confidence yet I shy away from him without wanting to. I thought I was at ease with another gentleman, Mr. McLaren. An incident yesterday, however, showed me how formidable and powerful a man he is. He is not only violent but the match of any three men. He has never given me reason to fear him personally, but I do anyway. I suppose what I fear is his strength. And for the first time I fear our situation. I had been led to believe we carried a shovel in our canoe for purposes of convenience and housekeeping. Yesterday Messrs. Mac-Pherson and Berelais dug a grave with it, its intended purpose all along. I am ready to abandon this whole quest. I never dreamed in starting that the cost would

*be so high. But Mr. Landry is eager to press on, so on
we press. Our forces are divided, however. The North
Wester André Berelais is taking the smaller of the two
canoes back to civilization. With him is Durwyn Sims,
who was injured. Mr. Sims feels he can still handle a
canoe, at least part of the time. They will take with
them an unfortunate old Indian woman we found. The
larger canoe will continue onward with Mr. Landry,
Mr. McLaren, Mr. MacPherson, Mr. Gibson, and
myself. I suggested that perhaps it would be best if
Mr. Gibson accompany the other party, but Mr.
Landry insists we need him, and that was that. And
Mr. McLaren will not part with his Wooly—that is,
Mr. MacPherson. This letter is being sent south with
Mr. Berelais. As it leaves here I am in good health. I
trust it will find you likewise. Plunging forward, I am*

> *Your dutiful niece,*
> *Linnet*

Linnet squirmed her bottom against a mossy stump
and leaned back against it. She took a deep breath and
closed her eyes. Amazing, that she should grow so
weary doing nothing more than simply sitting in a
canoe. Of course, when you sit in a canoe for nearly
three weeks running. . . .

They had come within inches of finding her father
not once, not twice, but three different times. When
would they realize they would not catch the fox?
Linnet wanted to go home. She did not want to watch
autumn close down this quiet country. She did not
want to sit forever in a bobbing canoe as chance after
chance slipped by.

The morning sun had warmed her face (and en-
larged her freckles, no doubt). Now the clouds had
moved in to protect her from the freckling and the
suntanning, and not because she wanted them to. She

yearned for some genuine penetrating warmth. Mr. McLaren insisted this chill was most unseasonal, but that made it no less chilling. She opened her eyes again.

Somewhere behind and below her crashed the stream—the ubiquitous howling, rushing stream. This bankside meadow stretched a furlong or two up and away from the water, a welcome gash in the dense dark forest. Earlier in the summer the meadow rippled with grass and wildflowers; the dying skeletons of Queen Anne's Lace put dark smudges into the smooth yellow-brown. No doubt the grass once whispered beneath the feet of deer and the teeth of hares. Already the meadow was falling asleep beneath a blanket of dead stems and grass. Once the meadow had shone glorious. It sulked now, somber, almost with a scowl of foreboding, and waited for winter to ruin it completely.

Gib had chosen this site, a flat grassy sward off to the side of the meadow. She noticed he always moved up and away from the stream channel. She noticed, too, that a cold breeze usually followed the rushing water along its way. Up here beyond that cold stream the air was at least a bit warmer. Give the devil his due—Gib certainly knew how to pick a comfortable resting place. He was watching her again. It made her skin prickle.

Simon sat on a weathered rock, his elbows on his knees, reading his Bible. He did that often and it seemed to annoy James no end. James's comments made it obvious that he thought Simon should apply himself constantly to the matters at hand and not be forever sticking his nose in a book. Gib and Wooly were both building a wall of pipe smoke between themselves and the lunch dishes. Despite James's words of praise all those many weeks ago, Linnet was getting heartily sick of dishwashing.

James had disappeared into the woods, no doubt on private business. Here he came back. Linnet almost smiled; she enjoyed just watching him. She did notice how dirty his clothes were becoming. That was most unlike him; he kept scrupulously clean those parts he could wash regularly. Yet, regardless these crude circumstances, he carried himself with the regal air of a prince of England.

Simon? Surely Simon's clothes were just as dirty, but the dark wool failed to show it. He marked his place with the ribbon now and sat erect.

"Gentlemen? Shall we be on our way?" James paused in the middle of the group and looked about. He turned to look squarely at Linnet. Those lovely eyes of his caressed her face and asked great favors of her. How could she resist?

She melted and stood up. "I'll clean up these few things. They'll be ready by the time you're packed up."

James turned to Simon. "The moon is coming full tonight. I think we should push on later into the evening. We're spending too much time sitting around fires and doing nothing. And as regards fires, I think . . ."

"Resting and doing nothing are nowhere near the same thing." Simon laid his Bible aside in the dry grass. "Handling the canoe in these sparse waters is hard work. Try to see the wisdom in pacing ourselves. We still have to get out of this country before snowfall, you know."

"But we could be doing so much better than this."

"Much better? No. A little better perhaps. We can push harder, but we'll pay a heavy price for every extra mile we stuff behind us. Besides,"—Simon stood erect—"distance isn't the issue. Our quarry is near; the trick is cornering him."

"Which brings me to my next point. Fires. We'll

make cold camps the next couple days. I can't see the use of advertising our presence with a column of smoke every night. We've been chasing our own tails for a month."

The bemused smirk was back on Simon's face. "Feel free to blow trumpets and set the meadow ablaze as you wish. They know we're here."

"Bosh! You can't presume to guess that we're not undetected. If we move fast and don't announce ourselves in any way . . ."

"*Mister* Landry!" Simon's voice did not really rise; it simply thundered at its normal volume. "I'm sure you know your way around the cobblestones of London. But you don't seem to grasp that out here you're as helpless as a blind dog in a busy street. We're in the middle of their territory. Of course they know exactly where we are."

"And we'd know exactly where *they* are if you hadn't sent that old woman off with her mouth still shut. Had you simply put the screws to her a little we wouldn't be chasing about blindly for a month. That was foolhardy of you to let her go when she could give us the information we need to end this matter promptly." His voice rose. "You know, McLaren, you've been a millstone around our necks this whole trip. I don't like your patronizing attitude toward me or Linnet. You never let her out of your sight, as if you alone stood between her and disaster."

"Perhaps I do. You don't seem to . . ."

"I can understand your reluctance to watch a fellow North Wester come to justice. But you know well he's a scoundrel, and you came along only to sabotage the enterprise. That makes you a scoundrel, McLaren." His eyes were firing darts at Simon.

And Simon's eyes were firing right back. He opened his mouth but . . .

Linnet let her stack of dishes drop. She heard at

least one break. It certainly caught their attention. "Stop it, both of you! The next moment one of you is going to offer to abandon the other, and the other will take you up on it. And then where will I be? Sitting in the middle of some forsaken meadow between Detroit and the North Pole, and that's about as close as I can pinpoint our position. We are on a cooperative venture, gentlemen, and we will cooperate—at least until we get back to something that passes reasonably for civilization." She glanced at Gib and Wooly. Their faces betrayed their thoughts—they both gleefully anticipated a fight. She snorted. "Mend your fences or not as you choose, but do hold your peace, both of you. I want to go home. I'm tired. I'll be waiting down by the canoe." She turned on her heel and marched off across the meadow.

Her eyes burned. She feared Simon but she liked him, too, very much. It was a strange sort of affection she could not begin to understand. He was a protector, a solid, dependable wall between her and the cruel world. He seemed to care about her in a fatherly way. She relished that—because she had never known a father's love or a father's protective hand, this feeling especially pleased her. But his anger angered her. And James? If half Simon's reputation as a fighter were true, James tangled with Simon at his peril. It didn't seem quite fair, either. James was so well muscled. And he was two inches taller, yards handsomer, probably younger by several years. . . . James. Why must he be so petulant at times, so insistent on his own way? James's dark side angered Linnet even more than Simon's anger did.

She turned her back on the lea with all its petty frictions to watch the stream roaring below. A bolt from the blue, a horse and rider came galloping out of the forest along the side of the stream. The rider wore a strange two-peaked white hat and dark capote—

Métis! Without slowing his horse he flicked a rope over the bow of their canoe. The horse thundered past it. The canoe jerked straight up on end; its nose pointed briefly skyward. Linnet heard the sharp crack as its back snapped. It dropped gunwales-down into the howling stream. The water snatched it instantly and hurled it out into the freshet. Swept up in the crashing current, it rushed away downstream upside down, circling about itself, bumping now and again against some shining rock.

The Indian wrenched his horse's head around and started up the bank! Linnet scooped up her skirts and raced back across the lea toward the safety of camp, toward the solid wall.

Three more riders burst full-tilt out of the trees, shrieking. A rifle blammed; a blue-gray cloud formed beside a rider; he left it hanging in the air as he rode on.

Gib was on his feet, his striped vest vivid against the brown grass. He swung the squirrel gun up. It disappeared in a cloud of smoke. Other guns fired. The several clouds melded into a single hazy pall. Gib dropped the rifle and yanked a pistol from his belt. Wooly stood near him; Wooly disappeared in a puff of gunsmoke.

Gib cried out and buckled over in the middle. His head bowed. Casually he dropped to his knees, all curled in a loop. Linnet stopped, fear-frozen. He didn't topple; he just knelt there, his forehead in the grass.

"Linnet!" Simon's voice shrieked, distraught. Ten feet behind Gib, Simon's pistol spit noise and orange fire and blue-black smoke. Wild-eyed he came bursting through the acrid cloud. He cast aside his spent pistol as he bolted toward her at a dead run. A rifle blasted beside Linnet's ear. Simon jerked to a stop in midstride; his arms flung wide, he pivoted a full turn and crashed backwards into the dying grass. Linnet wheeled toward the rifle sound.

Through the bitter haze she locked gaze with—with her own blue-gray eyes! The eyebrows arched just as her own; the beard was the coppery brown of her own hair. She knew him. Oh, yes, she knew him! He stared at her, transfixed, as his horse danced in place white-eyed. The spell broke. He swung the muzzle of his gun up and shouted something in French about breaking it off. He wrenched his horse's head away from her; his heels thumped in its ribs. He was gone. They were all gone. The endless meadow hung empty, engorged in silence, beneath that gray pall.

She tried to move and she could not. She tried to fold her knees and simply sit a moment; she could not.

Simon.

Simon had just died for her. Simon had just died trying to save her. If only . . . if only . . . she began sobbing, huge sucking sobs from deep inside. The sobs jarred her legs into motion.

She paused beside Gib as he melted quietly over onto his side, still all curled up. She jerked into motion again. On one knee, Wooly hovered over Simon. He had pulled Simon's coat sleeve off his left arm and was pressing both hands where the shoulder sloped up to meet the neck. Simon's shirt and tie were as bloody as Wooly's hands.

"Get 'is shirt off, lass, and his tie. Quick now!"

"Me? I . . ." She dropped to her knees beside Simon's head and tugged at the tie. "He's so white, he's almost blue. Is he . . . ?" The tie came free. Wooly grabbed it and squeezed it against Simon's neck. Cherry-red blood seeped up between his fingers. Linnet unbuttoned three buttons and yanked off the two that refused to come undone.

"Good enough, lass. Now go fetch the towels. All

of them. Then water in the shaving basin. Step quick now!"

She lurched to her feet and ran for the carpetbags. James was standing out in the open, trying to load the squirrel gun and watch the woods all around. He laid the squirrel gun aside and scooped Simon's pistol out of the grass. Linnet snatched the basin and ran down to the stream. By the time she got back with the water he was tucking the loaded pistol into his belt and reaching for another spent gun.

She folded her legs beneath her near Simon's head. She had to steady the basin on the uneven ground. Her mind and body were numb.

Simon mumbled something and stared blankly at Wooly a few moments. His eyes sparked to life. "Linnet. Get Linnet."

"She's fine, lad. Rest easy."

"She's in the open. She'll get hit." He arched his back, struggling to rise. His right arm flailed.

Wooly pushed him down flat. "I said it's over! She's safe. They're gone. Ye hear me?"

Linnet grabbed his right hand and squeezed it. "I'm fine. I'm right here. It's all over." She tried to smile at him, regretting her wild sobbing. Her face was all wet, her nose runny. Perhaps he would not believe that she was unharmed.

"Linnet . . ." He stared at her long moments, as if his brain were slow to register. His fingers curled around her hand and tightened a little. He sighed heavily. Again. His eyelids dropped to half-mast as he took long, slow gulping breaths. She clung to his hand and looked at Wooly.

"So far, not too bad." The bear flashed a momentary smile. "That gun packs enough wallop to drop a running buffalo in its tracks. We're lucky, lass. Muckle lucky."

"Lucky?!" Linnet shuddered and sniffed. The sobs

were finally subsiding. She twisted around to look at Gib. Gib wasn't dead. He moved slightly and moaned. James was crouched over him but he didn't seem to be doing much. In fact, James looked pretty much at sea. He raised his eyes to Linnet.

His look, his attitude, told her that nothing could be done for Gib. He didn't have to say so aloud. She clamped her lower lip in her teeth. Gib repelled her. He was boorish and crude and lustful. He threatened her; he frightened her. But she didn't want him to die!

Wooly glanced up at the sky. He looked at the treetops all about. Linnet's eyes followed his. The tall, pointy tips swayed casually in a restless breeze. She saw nothing unusual, except that the thin overcast had perhaps become heavier. Possibly the overcast was not thicker; she might simply be looking at it with eyes made murky by fear and worry. Gib. Simon. The canoe.

"The canoe is gone." Her voice trembled slightly. "Downstream. I think they damaged it."

Wooly looked at her. "Then I've a job for ye, lass. Walk a bit downstream and see if ye can find it—if it be hung up somewhere we can reach it."

She looked at Simon lying there so white.

"We need the canoe, lass. It's important."

She laid Simon's hand on his belt and climbed stiffly to her feet. No, she did not want to walk downstream. She did not want to leave this spot. She walked on sluggish feet down the hill to the stream. *We need the canoe, lass.* There was an urgency in his voice, a fear poorly masked.

She worked her way half a mile down the stream as the water crashed and gurgled and drowned out every other sound. She clambered over boulders and struggled over fallen trees. She went much further than she felt like going simply because it was Wooly who had asked her, Simon who needed her. No canoe.

The stream funneled into a narrow slot of bare rock. Steep ridges rose on both banks. Laughing exuberantly at its joyride, the splashing water rushed through the slot and cascaded out of sight. She couldn't go any farther without climbing this ridge-back. She peered as far as possible. No canoe. She turned back upstream.

She thought about her father's face. What had she seen in it before he met her eyes and gaped? Hatred? No, not really. Contempt. That was what she saw there. She thought about Wooly's face. There she had seen just the opposite—concern. Grim, urgent concern. Here was a hulking, clumsy bear who behaved toward Simon as tenderly as a mother with a newborn babe. And Simon? In the months she had known him he had spoken but a single word in frantic fear—her name. He had forgotten everything else, including his own safety, in his haste to save her. Now look! She was crying again. She wiped her wet cheeks fiercely, angry with herself for dissolving so easily at every random little thought.

Might the Métis return? Obviously James thought so, for he had made reloading his first priority. For some reason Linnet did not think so, but she couldn't find a reason for her feeling. Was that one distracted glimpse of her father the last she would have of him? What a horrible twist to her quest that would be!

She slogged up across the lea, through the brown and dying grass. Gib still lay where he had fallen but a point blanket was tucked in snugly all over him. James's rolled-up cutaway coat pillowed his head.

Simon, half-sitting and half-sprawling, was propped against a decayed stump. His coat had been draped over his bare shoulders. A little of the color had returned to his face but he was still pale. For the first time Linnet could see the extent of his wound. The lead ball had torn up that triangle of muscle sloping between shoulder and neck. An irregular blotch of bright red marked the exact spot. The blood smeared copiously elsewhere was turning dark. The bandaging wrapped snugly from his left neck and shoulder down under his right armpit. It was as tight as possible, obviously, but the bleeding had not entirely stopped. The bandage reflected the bear who had applied it— clumsy, bulky, dirty, and as effective as possible. Linnet thought Simon's left arm really ought be in a sling but she had no idea how one might fashion a sling. His thumb was hooked in his belt.

James squatted, balanced on the balls of his feet, near Simon's right. Wooly hunkered down Indian-style on the other side. This was no doubt a war council, a now-what-do-we-do? session. They watched her approach. Intensely bone-weary, she plopped in the grass near Simon's feet. She looked at Wooly and shook her head.

James snapped crossly, "Perhaps if you'd gone a little further . . ."

"I went as far as I could. The stream spills down through a narrow slot like this." She held up her arms.

"Ah!" Wooly nodded. "Then she went far enough. Either the canoe would hang up somewhere on this side of the drop or it's in wee pieces now. LeClerc Cascade will chew apart a dugout."

Simon's head sank back against the stump. He closed his eyes and sighed. Linnet wanted very much to hold his hand again, but she was too tired to move in closer. How she wished that the perfectly hand-some man shared Simon's steady disposition. Simon was frustrated by as many reverses as James was— more, even—but he never became short or crabby. Steady Simon, beautiful James—why was life always so complex? Why could perfection not be perfect?

She forced such comparisons out of her mind. They wearied her.

James rubbed his face with both hands. "There has to be a trail through here. The Métis can't get their horses through the woods without one."

"Trails aplenty, aye, but they won't take us anywhere we want to go. At least, not fast enough." Wooly looked at Simon. "Ye smell the wind?"

"Aye," Simon rumbled. "I smell it. Too early for this, Wooly. Too soon." He opened his eyes. "How about Dinwiddie Creek?"

"Nae, too far. Ten miles at least. Neither y'rself nor the lass'll make it. She's fair spent, and y'll not walk ten yards on y'r own, I aver."

"Smell what?" James asked.

"The sky, the wind shifting, the feel of the air." Wooly scratched his beard. "Storm brewing. We need good shelter and quickly."

James studied Simon's knees without seeing them. "The only place names I remember from company maps of this area are Bremington and Ainsley Houses, and I think they're both abandoned now."

"Ainsley!" Wooly snapped his fingers. "The very thing! I'd forgotten all about it. Lac Bouleau, less than two miles hence."

James looked at him listlessly. "Still more than the ten yards you just quoted."

Wooly heaved gracelessly to his feet and stretched. "Fifteen minutes to build a travois for Simon here. An hour to get there. We can make it. Y're brilliant, Jimmy m' lad."

"No." The dry rasp came from Gib's blanket, but it didn't sound a bit like Gib.

Gib's voice crackled, almost falsetto. "I don't want to die alone."

"We'll get Linnet and McLaren to safety and come

94

right back here for you. You won't be alone very long," James purred.

"No time. It's gonna be raining in an hour. Or snowing." The voice had disintegrated to a coarse whisper. "Please don't leave me to die alone."

"It's all right, Gib," James crooned. Even Linnet could tell from his smooth speech that it was not all right—not in the least.

"He goes with us." Simon's eyes were closed again.

James shook his head. "Not enough of us. We can't manage it."

"He's right. There's only time for one trip. We'll manage."

"I'm sorry, McLaren. We can't . . ."

"He goes!" Simon's tortured body might be pallid and motionless but none of the authority had leaked out of his voice.

James looked to Wooly for support. After all, Wooly was a true-blue North Wester and Gib a Bay boy.

Wooly nodded. "He goes." He wiggled a finger. "Help me, Landry. We'll be done shortly."

James patted the blanket. "The city boy yields. You go." He hopped to his feet and followed Wooly off into the woods.

Linnet gathered her skirt aside and scooted in close to Simon's right side. She scooped his hand into hers. The hand was cool and clammy; it had always been warm before. His knuckles were scarred white—from fighting in some distant past? It looked so. A puckered pink scar angled across the palm, obliterating his life line. She traced it with her finger. She glanced up.

He was looking at her. "Fort William. Knife fight with an Orkneyman nine years ago."

"Most soldiers collect battle decorations. You collect scars."

95

He smiled. "I wasn't a soldier then. Not God's soldier, that is. I came under His grace the following winter. Became a Christian in January of 1810."

"I thought we were all born either Christian or pagan."

"As regards heritage. But I've learned that faith itself requires that we each submit to God personally and individually. Heritage is our past. Conversion and submission is the present and future."

His brush with death had loosened his tongue. She did not care to talk religion just now. She switched subjects. "What does the future hold? I mean the immediate future?"

"I honestly don't know what God has in mind for us just now."

How might she phrase this? "Will you . . . ah . . . do you think . . . . ah . . . ?"

He smiled and squeezed her hand. "Heavy bleeders usually don't develop infections or tetanus, and the ball passed clear through. I'm lucky—especially considering the fact that I got hit with a buffalo gun."

"That's the second time I heard that. What about him?" She dipped her head toward Gib.

The smile fled. "The slug is lodged somewhere in his belly. He'll die in the next couple of days."

She whispered, "Should you be saying that aloud?"

"He knows. Some animals can survive being gutshot. A man can't."

She looked over at the motionless blanket. She felt suddenly drained, gray. Infection, fever, intense pain, the sure knowledge of death—and all that dragging on for days—the enormity of Gib's fate crushed her down. Her lip started quivering.

Simon disengaged his hand and laid it on the nape of her neck. He drew her gently against himself, pressed her head into his good right shoulder. He wrapped a strong arm around her back and hugged her in close.

"I'm sorry I let Landry bring you. I should have insisted that you remain behind at Cumberland House. We could just as well have brought your father to you."

She closed her eyes and snuggled in closer against him. "Did you recognize the man who shot you?"

He hesitated briefly. "Yes."

"So did I. So I suppose my quest is ended. I thought until now that James only wanted my father's help in finding the culprits of the Seven Oaks massacre. My father *is* the culprit, isn't he?"

"Landry thinks so."

"Do you?"

He hesitated longer. "Yes."

"I had such dreams," she murmured. "It was going to be such a bright adventure. Strenuous, yes. But noble and beautiful. And . . . and now look at it. Ashes. All of it ashes. My father is . . . and you are . . . and poor Gib there . . . and . . ." She ceased her talking. Words were sometimes so useless.

He rubbed the back of her shoulder a few moments, then ran his fingers up to massage the back of her neck. She felt so drab now, so spent, she couldn't even cry. Her happy world had shone bright yesterday. Today it yawned black and hollow. The only bit of brightness—the only speck of light—in the vast hollow void was the gentle touch of Simon McLaren.

CHAPTER 7

Dear Heavenly Father,
Dear God (or however You wish to be addressed),

I am aware that Simon McLaren is on much better
speaking terms with You than am I. You may note,
however, that he is unable to speak—to You or to
anyone else at the moment, so I shall speak on his
behalf. He looks upon You as some sort of benign
Father Figure. He follows Your rules and regulations
scrupulously without stumbling. He has controlled his
tongue, his temper, and his behavior according to
Your commandments (that is, Your commandments
as I know them, which I confess is not a thorough
knowledge). Therefore, I ask Your blessing on his
swift recovery. I do trust he will recover, as he is Your
faithful servant.

And another thing . . . to the best of my understanding Wooly is lax in such matters and James
shows no obvious interest in pleasing You either—at

*least not in the way Simon does. I am driven to ask: If
You are such a benign and loving Father, why did this
happen to him??!! I can see that Gib might deserve
some retribution (though not this hideous a punish-
ment surely), but Simon . . . Either You are a much
sterner disciplinarian than is called for, or You
possess a cruel and twisted sense of humor. In either
case, I cannot trust You and I don't understand how
Simon can. Yet he does. Restore Your servant Simon
McLaren. I am,*

Expectantly yours,
Linnet MacLeod

Sometimes the brightest gold in the world is simply
a day in waning summer. Tall swaying grass flows on
the open leas. Evergreen branches sport a million
brilliant green tips in the sunlight. The clear blue sky
washes pale with a gentle haze. Dragonflies sparkle
and butterflies flash bright colors, neither one aware
that the end of life is near.

But that was sometimes, in golden memories.
Today there was no gold, no brightness. The sky was
leaden, the meadows gray. Butterflies and dragonflies
had quit the field entirely. The glowering forest
enveloped Linnet in its dense and somber shade.
Midafternoon hung as dark as nightfall. A chill wind
rattled the treetops and penetrated to ground level
here. Linnet pulled her wool wrap close around, and
still she shivered.

A bear of ceaseless strength, Wooly dragged his
burden as if it were made of twigs and not stout green
poles. The travois was deceptively simple—two long
poles forming a narrow V with Wooly at their meeting
place. The nether ends bumped along the ground.
Between them, cross poles formed the bed to which
Simon was tied. The carpetbags, the ax, and a few

supply sacks were mounded up all around him; he could not have rolled off even if he were not tied down.

Wooly knew his way, following the streambank here and cutting across an open moor there. No doubt he was trying to select the smoothest possible route, but the travois bounced horribly all the same. Linnet followed behind it, watching Simon's face grow paler, his lips bluer.

Behind Linnet, James dragged an identical travois with Gib and the remaining baggage. Linnet appreciated James more and more with each torturous yard of travel. The man admitted freely to being a city fellow. Yet he took naturally to these backwoods skills. Even Wooly commented upon how quickly James picked up this and that. Now weary as he was, James slogged along with his usual victorious determination. His clothes were grimy; his beaver hat, fouled with everything from blood to mud. Yet he himself—the man—was as crisp and courtly as when Linnet first laid eyes on him. She admired immensely this elegance that was such a natural part of him and felt herself again softening in her opinion of him.

A cold raindrop splatted on her cheek. Another blipped on her eye, closing it momentarily. It was over now. It was all over. Simon and Gib would both get soaked through. They'd die for sure. How far yet . . .

"Hah! We made it!" Wooly crowed exuberantly.

Linnet moved a little aside to see ahead. They were entering another grassy clearing, a sward which sloped slightly down to a flat, lackluster little lake. Up at the far end stood Ainsley House—or what was left of it. The stockade had disintegrated to a couple of random, haphazard posts. The few buildings left standing were missing major parts, such as roofs and walls. The wasted ruin before them failed to crush

Linnet's spirits further simply because her spirits were already at their lowest ebb.

Wooly laid his burden gently on the ground and lumbered off, scouting. James wiggled out from under his travois and lowered it carefully. The rain was pelting down in earnest now.

He doffed his beaver hat and ran his fingers through his hair. "They warned me in London that I could expect new experiences. I don't think they realized just whereof they spoke."

"You're doing magnificently, James. A natural-born woodsman."

"Marvelous." His voice dripped sarcasm. "What a splendid life. No real mattresses, no clean sheets. I can't wait to get back, believe me."

"You're so certain we'll survive this."

"Of course we will!" He stepped over to her and gave her a cheerful hug. "You're my questing partner, remember? And I am invincible, though humble."

She gaped. The giggle exploded out of her before she could clap her hands across her mouth to catch it.

He waved a hand. "You know that southward extension of Hudson's Bay, don't you?"

"James Bay. But . . ."

"They were going to name it Landry Bay but I prevailed upon them. 'Please,' I said, 'something a bit less grandiose. After all, I am but a common man.' 'Very well,' His Majesty replied, 'James Bay, it is.' Humble, you see?"

For a moment—for a brief and shimmering moment—all the day's cares lifted away and hid themselves somewhere beyond feeling. She couldn't stop giggling. "Humble, my dainty foot!" she stammered. "Only royalty presumes to be known by the first name only. King George. Queen Elizabeth. Oliver. And now James. Humble, indeed! Obviously, it's only by a quirk of birth that Henry Hudson isn't employed by the Landry's Bay Company."

"What a clever girl you are! You're catching on. Hallo. Here's MacPherson back."

Wooly came waddling over. He picked up his load again. "Found just the place. Step lively now, Jimmy. We're nearly there."

" 'Step lively, Jimmy,' " James muttered.

Linnet smiled in spite of her weariness. She stumbled a little in the long wet grass. The coarse strands had fallen over in all directions. They grabbed at her ankles and the scratchy seed heads made her skirts all prickly. Wooly disappeared into a rickety cabin with half its roof caved in. She had to duck a slanting timber to enter the door, from dull gray into utter blackness. The dirt floor was powdery dry. At least they were out of the rain.

"We're not settled yet, Jimmy." Wooly stepped into the half light of the doorway. "Some thick bough beds—won't take long." James lowered Gib's travois, shot Linnet a weary glance and followed Wooly out.

Suddenly she was alone in the dark. Gib stirred and moaned; or was that Simon? Something skittered in a black corner. She sat down. She flopped over on her side and curled up on the hard ground, bone tired.

Gib buckled; Simon pinwheeled.

The vision robbed her repose. She shuddered.

A fire. They needed a fire to drive out the clammy cold in this forsaken hole. Every bone ached. Even her teeth hurt. Wooly and James both carried tinderboxes in their bags; most likely Gib did also. It wouldn't matter which bag she raided.

She sat up and rolled to her knees. She crawled three-limbed, one free hand pulling her skirt ahead of her knees, in the general direction of Simon's travois. She bumped into it in the the darkness and groped about for a carpetbag—any bag. Here was one. She opened it without releasing the ropes that lashed it down. Her exploring hands found . . . a candle. This must be James's. He was prepared for anything, yet she felt nothing in the bag resembling a tinderbox.

Her eyes were beginning to sort out gross shapes and shadows now. She heard either James or Wooly coming. A tall, lithe figure loomed in the doorway. He plopped a huge armload of green branches down and started back out.

"James? Do you have a tinderbox?"

He chuckled. "Where are you, fair lass?"

"Hiding in blackness as dark as my hopes, kind sir."

"Here now! Let's light a ray of hope. Keep talking." The figure started her way.

"I'm so tired I can't raise my eyebrows. I have never in my life been this weary."

He bumped into her. He knelt down, his leg against her. "Now for my bag."

"Right here."

He reached across her. His chest pressed against her shoulder and cheek. She closed her eyes and pressed back, hungry for any sort of comfort. The bag rustled. He sat erect.

"Better than a tinderbox by far. I just happen to have a candle here also." She felt his movement at her arm. "It's called an instantaneous light box. French invention. Marvelous piece. Here. Hold the candle, please." He *fwapped* the candle into her hand. She found the wick end by touch and held it up.

A flash of sudden brilliance startled her. He touched a flaming splint to the candle and grinned. "Let there be light . . . and there was light."

She wagged her head. "First you fancy yourself royalty and name bays 'James.' Now you fancy yourself God."

103

"Pity, isn't it—for in truth I'm neither. Jove, you look beautiful in this candlelight."

She was about to protest about her ragged, stringy hair; her soiled clothes; her dirty face. But then she realized he was quite as filthy, yet the dirt subtracted nothing from his charm.

He was looking at her with what Aunt Fearn would call calf eyes. Linnet preferred to identify his expression as rapt admiration. His eyes were asking questions and she was not about to shrink back this time. The answer to any question would be yes. He laid a hand on hers and they held the flickering candle together. With his knuckle he traced a line down her cheek. His fingertips followed the rim of her ear. He embraced the side of her head in his smooth, warm hand and drew it toward him.

She closed her eyes as his lips met hers. Why did one always close one's eyes during this most delectable of moments? And why should she possibly care why just now? She melted in against him and wrapped her free arm around his shoulder.

"Let me know when ye have a minute free." Wooly snorted. He dropped a load of branches and stomped back outside.

Linnet would have broken it off in embarrassment, but James's cupped hand prevented her. The kiss lingered. Eventually he moved away.

He smiled ruefully. "Duty calls at the most inopportune times. If you wish, just sit. We'll take care of things. Or gather some dry tinder and sticks. There's a fireplace against the wall"—he nodded toward the far side—"and I suppose it still works. Not plugged or fallen. I suspect it's only the fireplace which keeps this whole mess from coming down around our ears. We'd best get some warmth in here—warm up our two invalids. And you." He gave her a cheery little parting peck and patted her shoulder as he rose. He strode out the doorway.

Curious! If Gib, or any of her previous suitors, had patted her like that she would have turned purple. Yet she didn't mind it a bit coming from him. Would she mind if Simon did that? The question was immaterial; she could not imagine Simon's doing that.

He had given her a task, to gather. First she sat a few minutes savoring the rich memory of his kiss. He certainly knew his way around women. But then, so did Simon. The young men who had courted her in Detroit were so callow, so inept, so . . . so . . . Well, frankly, they didn't know the first thing about courting a girl. Kiss with a mouth shaped like a walnut? Hardly. She didn't realize back in Detroit, of course, that she didn't know a thing about it either.

Was James courting? Or was he simply a seizing the pleasure of the moment only? She guessed it was the latter, nothing more than a lark, but how ardently she wished he were considering courtship! And Simon? His one kiss had nothing to do with romance. It was a devious stratagem, a lie. And now that Gib no longer threatened there would be no more such stratagems. True, she occasionally noticed Simon's looking at her curiously. And he did seem to care about her. But it was a protective sort of caring, like a father for a child. Would she enjoy being courted by Simon McLaren? In a way. It might be interesting. Ah, but life with James would be intriguing. He was always reaching out, trying something different, learning something new. When she kissed James, she could kiss boredom good-by!

Stiffly she hauled herself to her feet. She dripped a little wax on the hearth and set the candle there. She found tinder aplenty; the dry bark was shredding away from the logs and roof beams. She garnered quite a pile of it in no time at all. Sticks were harder to find, particularly in this dim half light.

James popped in the doorway with still another great armload of branches. Those two must be denuding the whole forest! He looked at the hearth and rubbed his hands. "Splendid! Now you sit; I'll tend to this."

Gratefully she plunked down on the hearth and sank back against the cold, lumpy rockwork of the fireplace. James stacked the tinder and sticks, dripped some candle wax on the pyramid and lit it off. The fire flared up, crackling and welcome.

James thrust both hands very close to the flames. He toasted first the palms, then the backs. "MacPherson's bringing some dry firewood, he says. I have no idea where he intends to find dry stuff in that icy downpour out there. Of course, we're surrounded by dry firewood. Chop all the timbers we care to. Burn the house down here stick by stick, rather like Hansel's and Gretel's eating themselves into the gingerbread house, though in reverse." He frowned. "No, not like that at all."

Linnet giggled, too tired to simply smile. The brightness in the room now came from neither the candle nor the fire.

Wooly trundled in with still another armload of evergreen boughs. He brought half a dozen dry, dead tree branches to the fireplace and scratched his beard. "Fast work, for a city boy. Never saw a fire built quite so quickly."

"Instantaneous light box—an improvement on the old Italian pocket luminary. I'll show it to you then; uses chemical action to help ignite a splinter." James blew out the candle.

Linnet could see better now by the light of the growing fire. The cabin seemed pretty much intact at that end and a complete shambles at the far end. They were living inside a big triangle, for the wall and roof had collapsed completely at that far end, and the roof beams had fallen clear to the floor. The fireplace she leaned against was a heroic block of rounded boulders and small rocks stretching from the floor here past the darkness at the ceiling.

Gib on his travois still lay near the doorway, and there was Simon on his, the man completely obscured by parcels. No one had unloaded the baggage and Linnet did not feel the least bit like doing it herself.

Obviously James had made a bough bed before. Wooly hacked up the boughs and branches with flashing flicks of his big sheath knife. James laid large, thick branches width-wise and tucked soft little branches lengthwise among the larger ones. The big room filled with tangy tree-sap smell. Within a few minutes one bed was finished. James covered it with a point blanket and began the next. Linnet looked at the soft, inviting pallet and yearned to collapse on it. She must wait, for this one wasn't hers. She fed the fire Wooly's branches. It snapped and roared high.

The men made Gib as comfortable as possible over to the far right of the fireplace beyond the door. Gently they settled Simon into the bed nearest the fire. Wooly laid a heavy paw on Simon's neck and wagged his head. Even in this limited light Linnet could read the worry on his face. They built Linnet's bed near the fire also, and she was grateful. Wooly made his near the doorway, and James settled beyond Simon. By the time they were finished the mound of boughs was used up completely.

Wooly dragged out a pot and squatted at the hearth. Even pemmican sounded good to Linnet.

Wooly's head snapped around toward the entrance; he lunged for the squirrel gun. James snatched up a heavy stick and wheeled to face the doorway. Linnet's heart froze. Surely the Métis had tracked them here (No trick to that—even Linnet could track a dragging travois!) They were all trapped in here with no place to hide. Where was Simon's pistol? Linnet could fire a gun if she must. Or could she?

Gib buckled; Simon pinwheeled.

The interloper appeared in the doorway. He wagged his fuzzy loop of tail and came bounding across the room to Linnet. He tumbled into her lap and greeted her with slobbery kisses, all tongue.

She sat dumfounded a moment. "Mugwila's puppy! But how . . . ?" She looked up at the doorway.

That familiar wide form filled the patch of gray light. Mugwila seemed twice as wide as life, for her oiled doeskin rain cape hung like an ample tent.

"I don't believe it!" Wooly muttered. He lowered his squirrel gun.

Eyes snapping somewhere within those creases, Mugwila looked from face to face. She came marching straight across the room to Linnet and held out her hand. Nonplussed, Linnet reached up to her. Mugwila grabbed her arm and yanked her to her feet. Remarkably agile for so heavy a lady, Mugwila turned on her heel and started back toward the doorway, Linnet in tow.

"No!" Linnet finally realized Mugwila's self-appointed mission. "No!" She braced herself and jerked back, breaking free. Impatiently Mugwila grabbed for her again.

Linnet wrapped her arms around herself and stepped back quickly. "No, Mugwila, I can't go with you and leave these people. They're my friends. I . . . ah . . . Simon and Gib can't travel. Not now. I must stay with them."

Mugwila snapped something terse in Cree and held out her hand, insistent.

Linnet stared a moment at the work-worn hand. "I'm sorry. You came so far to help me. But . . . no."

She looked at the creases where Mugwila's eyes ought to be. "Gib is dying. Gutshot, Simon called it. And Simon might die, too. He was shot trying to protect me. To save me. I know you hate men, but these men need help and . . ." Struggling to frame her question, she chose a word or two from her sparse Cree vocabulary and, combining it with ample hand gestures, made herself understood: "You—Mugwila—stay here. Help us."

Mugwila spat out something derogatory. Linnet might not understand the words, but the tone of voice was clear.

Wooly was suddenly at Linnet's elbow. He crowded in close beside her and wagged a finger in Mugwila's broad face. "Now hear this, ye twice-fat harridan. Ye don't fool me with that Cree stuff. Ye know English as well as I do and French a whole lot better. I know ye do. I know ye understand every word she spoke. And she's right. I can't stand the sight of ye, ye wily old crone, and y'rself can't stand the sight of me. So be it. But we must both put ourselves aside. Gib's lost. But Simon's sinking and I don't know what to do for him."

Mugwila snarled something in Cree.

"That don't matter now," Wooly barked. "Ye can help him, I know ye can. And y'rself knows what sort of man he is. I won't despise ye any less three days from now, but I ain't too proud to beg y'r help now. M'self don't need ye and by the grace of God I never will. But Simon needs ye sorely."

Linnet stared at Wooly, open-mouthed. Mugwila glared at Wooly for long moments. She studied Linnet's face. She stared past Linnet so intently that Linnet turned to follow her gaze. James was hunkering down beside the fire, quietly scratching the puppy's thick fur with both hands. The puppy squirmed happily and pressed against his knee.

Wooly's voice dropped, softer. "Simon married y'r kind, and he loved her. He's a caring man, a giving man. He's not trash like most. Ye know that."

Suddenly Mugwila lurched forward, shouldering Wooly aside so roughly that the bear staggered back a step. She lumbered over to Simon's pallet and folded herself in the middle. Her legs still straight, she hovered close to his face. She laid her hands on him; lifted the blanket aside. She popped erect and spat out some derogatory word in Cree.

"Same to you, flea-woman!" Wooly walked back to the fireplace and propped the squirrel gun against the rocks.

Mugwila stood a few moments in the middle of the room, surveying the scene. She snorted. She waved an arm toward the doorway and spoke. She waved her arms toward Linnet and spoke. She pointed at James and spoke. She waddled off outside. The puppy bounded out the door after her.

"Orders, orders, orders. Makes Napoleon look like a blinking choir boy." Wooly scowled at the empty doorway. "If it wasn't for Simon . . ." He snorted. "She says we're to cover the doorway to keep out the wind. Says it's gonna snow tonight. She says you're to curl up in that bed by the fire and get some rest, lass. Claims ye look like y've been dragged through a hollow log. And she wants Landry to help her with her baggage. She's got two *pieces* out there."

James paused beside Linnet on his way out the door. "By a long shot I'd rather haul baggage for Napoleon."

CHAPTER 8

> *Ainsley House,*
> *September 18, 1818*

Dear Aunt Fearn,

We have located your brother. He is alive and well. I shall save the description of the meeting for when we meet again as it is too lengthy to detail here. I pray that will be soon, for I am ready to quit this country. We are for the moment

Linnet laid her pen aside and flopped down on her back. The green boughs beneath the blanket rustled and wheezed. For twenty-two years she had been Linnet MacLeod. She had always been proud of the name, proud of her Scots blood, simply because she had no reason not to be proud. Now she had ample reason to hide her head in shame. Her father was a murderer and a renegade, responsible for the massacre of twenty-two persons that Linnet knew of. When Gib died that number would be twenty-three, and if Simon died . . .

111

Gib buckled; Simon pinwheeled.

She covered her face with her hands for a moment. She opened her eyes again to stare at the dim sloping timbers overhead. Were she a man she would be stuck with *MacLeod* for life. But she could marry and leave that accursed name behind. Quitting the name would change nothing—not really—but at least she would no longer live under its shadow. She sat up and wearily massaged her forehead.

Wooly squeezed through the makeshift door with an armload of firewood. He waddled over to the hearth, stacked the wood, and began poking at the fire.

"Good morning, Wooly."

"Morning, lass!"

"I looked at Simon when I first woke up. His color seems better. And he seemed to be sleeping peacefully."

The bear wagged his shaggy head. "That woman's got a touch, lass. Bet I know how she stopped the bleeding. She stared at the wound with those cold hard eyes and scairt it to death. Even when he was moving around some early this morning, he wasn't bleeding. Aye, she put some color in his cheeks. And he was talking to me this morning with all his wits together. The obnoxious old crone's got a rare gift. Knew she could do it."

Linnet smiled at the awe in the bear's voice. "Wooly? The first night we met, at Cumberland House—remember?"

"Aye." He poked vigorously at the fire.

"You said I was more than you cared to tangle with. Why?"

He started to look at her but his eyes fell away. "Y'r father's reputation, lass, a reputation for going off half-cocked. He'd be bound to learn y'r up here. And he just might be sorely disposed toward any man who as much as looked as though he were taking advantage of ye."

"So to avoid my father's possible wrath, you quickly passed me off to Simon."

"Simon is Innis MacLeod's better. I'm not." Wooly grunted. "I daresay Simon's one of the few men between Hudson's Bay and Athabasca Lake who can match y'r father fist for fist, skill for skill. And he knows it."

"So that's why no one would talk to me about my father. No one wanted to be the one who told me what he is. They're all afraid of him." She glanced toward the pallet by the fire. "All but Simon." She watched the crackling fire a bit. "Wooly, why did my father attack us yesterday?"

The bear shrugged. "Got wind we're after them, mayhap. Decided to get the drop on us and deny us any chance of taking them unawares. Surprise attack is a great military advantage, ye know."

"I asked you because I want to know, not so I can get a pat answer."

Wooly studied her a moment. "Ye come a thousand miles to learn about y'r father and here I sit, fearing to tell ye. Fie on me! Mugwila told me last night that the word's spread all through the woods: Landry is out to catch y'r father and drag him off to England to hang for that massacre. The word claims Landry has a paper from the crown, Bay Company approval, and the blessing of the governor."

"I think it's true."

"The story has it he's using a girl who poses as Innis's daughter, as bait. That's not true. But it puts y'r life on the line. It makes ye no better than a Bay company foxhound, ye see."

"But my father knows now I'm for real. I saw the look on his face. I'm sure he recognized me."

"We can't count on it. Y'r life isn't charmed yet.

Mugwila heard by the gossip coming back that the Métis weren't about to let Landry get near Innis. The Métis were going to nip this bit of trouble in the bud.''

"And Mugwila, afraid for my life, came to find me and take me back to Cumberland House, out of harm's way. What a noble gesture!''

Wooly snorted. "Surprising how fast the old bat found us. She stumbled across Durwyn, André, and that old woman within four days of when they reached the fort. She put two and two together and ended up missing the party yesterday by less'n an hour. She could hear the gunshots.''

"That's right; she knows this area. Does my father know Simon is with us?''

"Don't know, and it don't matter. They might both have been North Westers together—and friends, once upon a time—but when Simon joined in with Landry that put him on the Bay side of the fence. The enemy side.''

"But to shoot him. . . .''

"Y'r father'd as soon shoot his own mother if she worked for the Bay.'' Wooly's eyes dropped, the thick eyebrows ruffled. He looked squarely at her. "Y'r father is who he is, lass. None of this—the shooting, the seeking, none of it—is y'r own doing. Y'r father was the best of the North Westers once, 'til he let the rivalry get outta hand. He makes himself the best at anything he does, and that's not a bad thing in a man. Take pride in that. Here now! Mugwila's made breakfast—cornmeal mush with weeds—and she says y'rself is to eat plenty. She opines as y've lost weight.'' He waved toward the pot on the hearth.

"*Bon appetit!*'' He jerked to his feet and shuffled outside.

Linnet sat alone in the near darkness. Why couldn't these fur traders build cabins with windows? Of course, had there been windows the walls probably

114

would have collapsed completely. She stuffed two logs on the fire, although one would have been ample. It might be dark but it was toasty warm in here. She would have to abandon the warmth temporarily, though. Nature called. She threw her wrap around her shoulders and stepped outside.

A white swirl blinded her. She squinted until her eyes adjusted to the brilliance. Everything was white, a rather gray and dirty white. The snow was just barely clinging to things above ground level. Most of the flakes melted the moment they touched anything solid. The wet snow flashed past her face, driven on the wind. To avoid being blinded in a whiteout, she kept one hand on the cabin logs as she walked around back.

Linnet was outside only a minute or two. Yet when she ducked back inside, she was frosted with fluffy wet flakes. She bent over and brushed them off her head. She shook out the wrap and spread it across a log to dry. Sitting down on the hearth, she stared at the mush. Hungry as she was, it didn't look edible. There were James's fancy plates, stacked beside the rockwork. She plopped some of the sallow goo on one of the plates and picked up a spoon. She poked at it. She nibbled. It tasted like paper.

Simon's bough bed rustled. Grateful for the excuse to abandon breakfast, she put down the plate and crossed over to him. She plopped down beside him. "Good morning."

"Good morning."

"Would you like your reading glasses?" She glanced around. If she was going to offer them it would be nice for her to find them.

He smiled. "I know what you look like. I can describe every freckle on your face. I'd like the mug there, though. Whatever that is."

She picked up his drinking mug and swirled it a

little. Compared with this gray-brown fluid, the cornmeal mush looked absolutely delectable. "What is it?"

"I have no idea. Some product of Mugwila's alchemy."

"You must be terribly thirsty to want to drink this. Very well. Here."

He propped clumsily onto his right elbow. She steadied him with one hand and the mug with the other. She expected any moment to spill the whole putrid-looking mess down the front of his shirt. Exhausted by the exertion, he lay back and drew in a few deep breaths. Should she sit here or go elsewhere? She didn't want to intrude on his rest, but she didn't want to leave, either.

"You were talking to Wooly a few minutes ago."

She smiled, happy to talk. "I hope we didn't wake you."

"You didn't. I've been drifting in and out all morning. You didn't know your father at all, did you?"

She shook her head. "I was so small, and he was around such a short time."

"Do you remember anybody's loving father at all? A friend's? Some affectionate uncle or other relative?"

Linnet drew her knees up to use as a chin prop. "There was Mr. Hartman, the shoemaker down the street. Aunt Fearn and I cleaned house for him. But he doesn't really qualify. I didn't know him well. Besides, he died before I was fifteen."

"You and your aunt are charwomen by occupation?"

"And very good ones, if I may say so. When someone sends Aunt Fearn in to clean, the dirt clamors to escape out the back way. Aunt Fearn commands top price, and I'm developing something of a similar reputation.''

The baritone chuckle was back to full depth. The strength in his voice delighted her.

She frowned. ''Why did you ask about—well, about substitute fathers?''

''Just thinking. I don't . . .''

Gib rasped something unintelligible from across the room. Linnet laid her hand on Simon's, a parting gesture, and crossed the room to Gib. She dreaded this; she had no idea what to say to a dying man. He was curled up on his side, his knees tucked in high. For all she knew, he had not moved from that position since he went down.

Gib buckled; Simon pinwheeled.

She sat near him and laid a hand on his shoulder. She closed her eyes; she couldn't look at him.

''Another blanket.'' His tongue slurred thickly.

Linnet hopped up and snatched the blanket off her own bed. She tucked it around him, doubled. It was his third layer of doubled blankets in a room already quite warm. He shuddered. From somewhere within the mound of wool came the vague and misty smell of warm sewage, of decay. Bereft of words, she laid her hand on the back of his neck.

She gasped and called across to Simon, ''Is there any way to relieve his fever? He—he's very hot.''

''Cold packs of snow and towels.''

She rubbed Gib's shoulder. ''I'll be back directly!'' Two towels hung drying on a slanted beam. She snatched them away half-wet and hurried outside. Not enough snow stuck to the ground to permit gathering. She brushed wet puffs off the bushes and trees. It took a few moments. She folded the towel-packs and hurried back inside.

In the doorway she stopped. She should complete her mission. Instead she stood watching. Gib's gravel voice was rattling something and Simon was rising from his bed. She shouldn't allow this; he was much too weak. In stocking feet he padded across the room like a ninety-year-old invalid and sat down very close to Gib. He wrapped his good right arm across Gib's shoulder. Linnet stepped into the warmth and listened.

". . . seeing you're a religious man," Gib was rasping. "Nothing fancy. You know, a prayer maybe . . . something from the Bible."

"The weather's cooled off considerably. We can probably get you to Carlton House if you'd rather be buried there."

"Don' bother. Here's all right. Don' matter where I am now."

"But it will matter a great deal after you die."

"You mean heaven or hell? I made my bed in hell. I know it and I'm ready to take it." Gib snuffled, a strange sound. "Always wanted to die glorious. Not like this. Not rotting slowly. Do great things. Make a big name. But I never had no illusions about going to heaven."

"Bet you had quite a father when you were growing up."

Gib chuckled. "Paw? What a man. Trapped a bobcat by a hind leg one winter. Wrassled that cat and wrenched its neck barehanded. That's the man my father was. Ain't men like that no more. You 'n' MacLeod come closest, but even you woulda never matched Paw."

"Whip you much?"

"All the time. But I deserved it."

"You're saying, then, that he disciplined you out of love."

"Yeah. Guess you could say that. He wouldn't know how to say he loved us, but he made us toe the

118

mark every minute we was in his house. That's love, ain't it?"

"He that spareth his rod hateth his son. But he that loveth him chasteneth him betimes."

"Bible."

"Proverbs. Yes. And in Hebrews it says, in effect, to rejoice when you are disciplined because it means you are loved. The Father loves you."

"Yep. That was Paw."

"Fathers here on earth are meant to teach us something about our Father in heaven. Earthly fathers have their faults, of course, but the heavenly Father doesn't. Perfect love, perfect grace, perfect mercy. Perfect forgiveness."

"Forgiveness?" Gib grunted. "Too late. I knowed right and wrong—Paw drummed that into me—and I never did enough right to make up for all the wrongs. Drunks, fights, women, cheatin'." The voice faded to a gritty whisper. "Never stole, though. Not a *sou*, I'm proud of that. But cheatin'? Don't ever get in a card game with me."

"Yes. The Father already figured you can't balance out all that. So He did it for you. His Son never once sinned but God let Him die anyway—to pay for everything you can't pay for. You don't have to take it in hell forever if you don't want to. He's giving you a way out."

"Wish it was true."

"It's true. You believe it's true and ask the Father to forgive you. He makes you His own—forever."

Linnet yearned suddenly to touch Simon. She felt incredibly alone. How else did she feel? She had to think about that a moment. Cheated. She felt cheated. A sense of loss engulfed her. Gib's father was hardly a loving patriarch, and yet how warmly Gib spoke of him! Gib cherished memories of a father who must have been brutal. Obviously a father was far more than just the man who headed up the family. There was so much more to a father, and Linnet had none of it. Gib remembered beatings; Linnet didn't even have that much to remember. The empty spot that plagued her so, deep inside, was father-shaped. It could be filled only by a father. The feeling depressed her more than she could say.

Gib snuffled again. Linnet realized he was chuckling. "Remember the big Canuck? With the ear cut off? What was his name?"

"Dalles DuBois." Simon chuckled also, tickled by the common memory.

"Yeah, that's him! I was one of them who watched you fight him. I had three beaver pelts riding on DuBois. It was only logical, right? He outweighed you by a hundred pounds. Never guessed I'd lose my bet. I'm just a dumb Welshman, but I learn fast. I never bet against you again and I never lost again. But you quit fighting. Got religious and quit drinking and turned around. Musta been hard for you. You're the best." The voice gritched like a carpenter's saw. Gib paused a few moments. "Wish I had time to change. I know it sounds like boasting—like a man who's desperate to make things up. But I mean it. I'd change today if I could. Like you did."

Silence.

Simon looked over at Linnet so she stepped forward. He glanced at the towels and shook his head. Quietly she dumped them out through the doorway and hung them back up to dry.

Gib buckled; Simon pinwheeled.

Drained and shaken, she collapsed her knees and squatted, as close to Simon as she could get.

Gib took a deep breath and continued. "Chubby little blond kid. Forget his name; they call him Lemming. He gets five. Cyrus oughta have five or six. Whatever's left. Got that?"

120

Simon nodded. "Your cache is on the south side of Chien Lake near the black rocks. Four made beaver go to Porky, three to each of your chums at Cumberland, two to the Kraut, five to Lemming, and what's left to Cyrus."

"Right. I owe more'n just them, but it's a start. Where's MacLeod's girl? Tell her I'm sorry. I shouldn't've tried for her. She's clean and I wanted to dirty her. So many people I have to ask to forgive me . . ." The voice failed.

Linnet's hands were shaking so violently she couldn't hold them still. She clamped her upper teeth over her knuckles. That didn't work either.

Gib's hand came creeping out from under the pile of blankets. The sinews traced deep ridges across the back of it, making it look all the more gaunt. Simon gathered it up in his good hand. The putrid smell was much stronger now that the blankets had moved. Linnet's chest felt heavy. Her eyes burned. Simon should be in bed now—his face was turning white again. Instead he sat here holding Gib's hand; Gib had begged that he not die alone. It was probably not important to Simon but it was to Gib. And that made it important enough to suffer for. Linnet tried to think about fathers, but nothing happened. She had nothing to think about. Her eyes overflowed.

Gib whispered. "You sure I'm His? I didn't have time to change like you did."

"Remember the story about the thief on the cross? You hear it every Easter." Simon's baritone was a whisper also.

Gib smiled grimly. "Yeah. That's me." Linnet realized it wasn't a smile. The corners of his mouth tilted up; that was all. His labored breathing was now louder than his voice. His breath smelled like dead rats. His hand and his body vibrated, rigid.

Gib buckled; Simon pinwheeled.

She buried her face in Simon's arm. It would all be over soon and the haunting vision would fade. Gib's suffering was ending now. Simon was recovering. Linnet could put her father's hideous work behind her soon now, and sponge the memory from her mind.

Gib buckled; Simon pinwheeled.

She sobbed.

The doorway scraped and rattled. Wooly's footsteps and James's. Wooly's stopped. Stricken, he muttered, "God bless the lad."

James crossed to the fireplace without pausing. He dumped a load of firewood; it clattered and clunked against the hearth. Linnet jumped and darted a hard look at him.

He stood erect and stretched his back. "No rest for the weary, I see. Now there's a grave to dig." As cheerful as ever, he brushed his hands off and strolled back outside.

CHAPTER 9

Dear Aunt Fearn,

I started a letter a few days ago and failed to finish it. In it I told you that as regards my quest, we have found your brother. I will give details about the meeting when I see you. Mugwila is here (my landlady from Cumberland House) but hers is a very small canoe, holding at most two people. Therefore, two of us will be leaving Lac Bouleau here (or Ainsley House, if you choose to give names to fallen facilities) and the same will bear this letter on its way, hopefully toward civilization.

Poor miserable Gib died on Friday and they buried him in the evening, which was as soon as they could get the grave dug. The expedition's only shovel apparently went over LeClerc Cascade still lashed to our canoe, but Wooly MacPherson fashioned a makeshift implement from a tin plate. The ground is not frozen here yet. Mr. McLaren preached a lovely

*funeral, according to Gib's wishes. I wept through-
out. They piled a huge stack of boulders on the grave
lest wild beasts disinter the poor fellow. The mix of
civil and savage, crude and refined, is both fascinat-
ing and confusing. The contrast of a Christian funeral
(which would pass muster in the largest city church)
with the threat of wild animals is only one example.
The men themselves are likewise—civilized gentlemen
one moment and part of this wild land the next. The
wind has calmed somewhat and the snow is ended.
Mr. McLaren will be able to travel soon, he claims.
I'm not sure; he preached the funeral sitting down.
With hopes of returning to you soon, I am*

> *your niece,*
> *Linnet*

Linnet stacked the clean dishes beside the rockwork and turned the last of the mugs upside down
beside them. She hung the dishtowel on a sloping
beam to dry. Now what? Wooly was stuffing dry
leaves in his little pipe, preparing another of those
obnoxious smokes. Simon had fallen asleep. She
studied James a few minutes, one of her favorite
pastimes. He was repacking his bag for the umpteenth
time, even though he'd not unpacked it today.

She smiled at a sudden brilliant idea. "That's what
needs be done! And I'm thoroughly qualified to do
it."

"You are thoroughly qualified for far more than you
realize." James looked up. "What do you have in
mind?"

"Your clothes. The ones on your back and the ones
in your bag. Laundry. Also Simon's shirts, both of
them, then my dress here. Whoever leaves here
tomorrow shall leave in a state of cleanliness. I have
this urge to be a washerwoman." She glanced at

Wooly. "Not you. I have no idea how one would go about washing buckskin."

Wooly chuckled. "Ye don't wash it, lass. Ye scrape off the top layer with sandstone."

She sniffed. "I was afraid it was something like that. Very well. You first, James. It's so warm in here they should dry in a few hours."

He set his carpetbag aside. "No washtub."

"My aunt and I can wash draperies in a bowl if need be. The shaving basin will do. Yellow soap in my bag—and there's enough water around to float an ocean ship."

He smiled and stood up. "You want everything?"

"Everything dirty. And that's everything."

He slipped out of his cutaway. "You have a rare gift for understatement. I feel like a walking cesspool." He unbuttoned his waistcoat and shirt.

Linnet dug her soap out of her bag, suddenly very pleased with herself. She could do something for James that he appreciated, and it was something she did well. He was by nature a very tidy person, as was she. She could understand how uncomfortable he must feel in grimy clothes. Not only was she performing a well-received service, he was bound to be impressed with her.

Did she want to impress him? Oh, yes! She didn't have to think twice about that!

He peeled the shirt off. His pale skin stretched firm around bulky shoulder muscles. He might be a city boy, but he was certainly no scrawny fop! He hesitated a moment, then scooped the blanket off his bed. "No peeking." He moved to the far end of the room and crouched under the slanting roof to complete undressing. He returned in moments with the blanket wrapped demurely around him. "You didn't peek."

"No, I didn't. You're such a handsome fellow, too."

"A brilliant opportunity lost." He flopped down on his bed and stretched out, all modestly wrapped.

Promising clean clothes and delivering them were two different things. Linnet had forgotten that the water wasn't as hot as it ought to be, for she could heat it only a kettle at a time. Just scrubbing James's clothes took the better part of an hour. She wanted to make certain all was spotlessly bright. He would hardly be impressed with a job only half done. She gave the trouser seat a final rubbing and held them out at arm's length for one more examination by firelight. She flopped them a double turn and twisted.

Wooly snickered and tapped his pipe empty on the hearth. "Let me give 'em a wring, Lass." He wrapped his bulky paws around the sopping cloth and wrenched away. The trousers, as dry as Linnet could wring them, gushed water into the basin. She had almost forgotten how powerful this stocky man was. Yet he rated his strength as second to Simon's.

Did James possess that kind of strength? Linnet had never seen his strength really tested. But the fleeting view she enjoyed of the man's shoulders and arms suggested he might. How important was physical strength? All sorts of strange little thoughts and questions skipped through her mind as she shook the trousers out, smoothed them, and hung them. Then all thoughts of James fled.

Simon's ruined shirt had been soaked thoroughly. If any of that mess was going to wash out of it, it would now. Yet Linnet dreaded tackling the job. More than once she had helped Aunt Fearn clean up the bloody aftermath of a childbirth. When Aunt Fearn left the house behind her, the mother was clean, the baby was clean, the house was clean. Aunt Fearn and Linnet as well were much in demand for that particular service.

Linnet had pretty much associated bloody messes with the arrival of new life.

Perhaps that's what made this different. The loss of this blood had been life-threatening and very nearly life-taking. The odor itself was different. She had to steel herself to touch the shirt, to drop it in the bowl. She had to fight herself, force herself to scrub the stains. She paused a moment to finger the big tear near the collar. Some of the ragged edges were scorched, as if touched by fire. She had heard that rifle balls became very hot as they flew through the air, hot enough to scorch—she shuddered. This ragged rip would be difficult to mend. She'd have to take a patch from the longest part of the shirttail there. She went back to rubbing.

And all this was because of her. Had she simply fallen forward in the scratchy grass and covered her head, she would have looked safe enough. Simon would have remained behind his tree, or wherever he had been. This misfortune would never have happened. She thought of the wild anguish in his voice when he cried out her name.

Gib buckled; Simon pinwheeled.

Would James have placed himself in harm's way like that for the sake of Linnet's safety? Certainly he would. He was a true gentleman. The only reason he did not was because Simon was there first.

Gib buckled; Simon pinwheeled.

She clamped her teeth over her lower lip and kept scrubbing.

Simon was still asleep when she finished his shirt and hung it to dry. It was not at all clean, but it might be usable again after mending. She would wash his other shirt later, after this one was mended. She dug into her bag and brought out the rolled muslin dress. She certainly couldn't wash clothes with a blanket wrapped around her.

She glanced at James. He was smiling and watching her as a cat watches a bird. She gestured toward him with the rolled-up dress. "This is going to hurt me more than it hurts you. But I know better than to bother asking you not to peek."

He sputtered an insincere protest as she stepped outside. As quickly as possible she slipped out of her warm, comfortable woolen dress and into the cold, flimsy muslin one. How ridiculous was this latest turn of events! After wearing loose wool all summer, here she was putting on a lightweight little number as snow and icy rain fell all around her ears. She shook her head and tied the sash at the back, up high. She scooped up her woolen dress and hurried back inside. She ran right to the hearth before she paused to shake the cold wetness out of her hair. She was shivering already, and understandably so.

James sat up. The blanket fell away from those marvelous shoulders. "Had I known you would go to such hideous lengths, I would have been a good boy. No peeking. Really, Linnet, you should have said something. And look! You're human, after all! Not just a fragile butterfly still encased in that limpid wool cocoon. Linnet, you're gorgeous. After this, stick to your own good fashion sense and ignore McLaren's stodgy suggestions."

She shook her head. "I might not have been your idea of loveliness, but neither was I victimized by all those mosquitoes. Even a cocoon has its use."

"But it deprives me of an absolutely heavenly vision. From now on, wear that dress and I'll swat the mosquitoes."

She laughed, not at him but at herself; she had found herself actually considering his flippant suggestion for a moment!

With a happy yelp the puppy burst through the doorway. Linnet paused a moment in her scrubbing to

128

scratch behind his ears. Mugwila waddled in and stopped. She scanned the hanging laundry, Linnet's ridiculous attire, James in his blanket. She snorted and dropped her burden basket down beside the rockwork. She snapped something antagonistic at Wooly.

"'Cause I don't have no sandstone, that's why." With a scowl he began packing his pipe again.

Linnet giggled.

Mugwila looked at Simon and spoke in Cree.

And Simon replied—in Cree! Linnet gaped. She wasn't surprised that he had awakened; he was bound to sooner or later. And she shouldn't be surprised that he knew the language. He had spent years in this country as a trapper and agent. Still the exchange startled her. To this moment Mugwila had spoken only to Wooly and then only in a hostile manner. Her voice toward Simon was tender. This woman who hated men was being amazingly polite, even caring, toward Simon McLaren. What did they say? It was none of Linnet's business and she would not ask. But sheer curiosity tickled her all the same, for it did not at all sound like the usual "how-do-you-feel"–"fine" exchange.

Mugwila bent double near the hearth and began laying out in piles the many plants and twigs she'd gathered.

Wooly took a long draw on his pipe and watched the smoke float ceilingward. "Out gathering more of them noxious sticks and branches. If man was meant to browse wood he'd have teeth like a moose's. Y'rself has the face but not the teeth. What's all these dead leaves and sticks supposed to do for us, anyway?"

Mugwila paused from her sorting to berate Wooly a few moments. She rattled off a long list of syllables as she pointed from pile to pile.

"Doubt it's gonna do any of that," he retorted, "except maybe make the tea a frightful color. Ye got a good look at the northern sky in y'r ramblings. What's it say to ye for tomorrow?"

She replied in one word.

"Ah, then we can be off early. Whaddaya think? Three days to reach Carlton House?"

She hooted and grunted something Cree and gutteral.

"Izzat so?! Day and a half, if I don't have y'rself to slow me down."

Linnet glanced at Simon. That happy look of bemusement was back on his face, the first she'd seen it in days. It delighted her. He struggled to sitting and slipped his glasses on, so apparently he intended to remain erect awhile.

"What say, Simon?" Wooly waggled his pipe in the air. "The crone and m'self, making fast time, back here in six days with canoes and reinforcements."

Simon shook his head. "Hate to break up such a charming match, Wooly, but we need you here. We're out of food and you and Mugwila are the only two people who can keep us fed. We need a reliable hunter who can bring home meat in good weather or bad. Landry here can't read sign if the weather drives game back into hiding, and he doesn't know what's edible out there and what's not. Landry and Mugwila."

"And leave you here alone with her?" James pointed toward Linnet. "Never!"

"I value propriety as much as anyone." Simon's voice was back to its old rumbling strength. "But propriety takes the hindmost in this situation. I can't paddle and Linnet isn't strong enough to make a good run. You're strong and you learn quickly."

"With that woman? Come now, McLaren!"

Simon was absolutely smirking. "I'd say you're both safe."

"But Linnet's not."

Simon's face hardened from bemused to grim, even angry. Linnet happened to glance at Mugwila. She glowered at James as if the man had just desecrated God, mother, and the flag. Linnet's heart jumped. She realized just then that James was making noises like a jealous man. Catty woman that she was, the thought struck her fancy. She found herself reveling in his jealousy for her. She scrubbed at her dress happily, paying absolutely no attention to what she was doing.

James slammed his fist into his knees in frustration. "I don't like it."

"Neither do I, particularly if the Métis decide to come finish the job while Wooly's miles away prowling after game."

Too agitated to sit, he suddenly leaped up, nearly courting disaster with that loose blanket. "This is a preposterous situation! You tell me the canoe holds only two. I have no idea if that's true or if you're stringing this city bumpkin a glorious line. Frankly it looks just like every other canoe in this forsaken country. You tell me this person should stay and that I should go. For all I know it's smooth sailing from here to there—or perhaps totally impossible to get there from here. I have no way of evaluating your grand assumptions."

"That's true." Simon lay down again and stretched out. "We can lead you about as if you wore a ring in your nose, and you've no way of catching on until after the fact—if at all. It's a position I've found myself in more than once. Frustrating. You have only my word that we're being forthright with you, but you do have that."

"I'm delighted you sympathize, but you've told me nothing." James paced back and forth in high dudgeon. He stomped over to the beams and snatched up his clothes.

"Those can't be dry yet!" Linnet protested.

"Then I'll stand next to the fire until they are," he snapped. "And I'm exercised enough that I don't give a fig whether you peek or not."

"Good! Then it won't disappoint you when I turn my back!" His crossness made Linnet angry. He had neither need nor right to snarl at her. She wasn't responsible for his—what did he label it?—"Preposterous situation." She saw no cause to doubt Wooly or Simon. They knew this country. On the other hand they could indeed say just about anything they wished. He was brand-new around here. Even Linnet knew more about the climate and the land than he did; at least she lived in Detroit. Mugwila's canoe was certainly much smaller than one of the freight canoes; she could portage it herself, and the north canoes required two men. But was her canoe so small Linnet could not go? Linnet wanted so badly to get back to some semblance of civilization. She didn't want to sit here for a week with nothing to do when she could sit behind James and watch his magnificent shoulders work. Could he handle a canoe? Of course. He could do anything he put his mind to. What a gift.

Mugwila didn't seem to like the suggested arrangement any more than James. She scowled contemptuously at him and clattered away in Cree. Both Wooly and Simon were answering her.

But James was studying Linnet. She returned his gaze for a moment and turned back again to the soapy water. What could she read in his face? She couldn't tell. Apparently he wanted something that he could not have; she could read that much.

She knew what Aunt Fearn would be saying right now. Aunt Fearn would describe in no uncertain terms exactly what James wanted. And Linnet no longer believed a word of Aunt Fearn's warnings. According to the picture the old spinster painted, all men were exactly alike—humorless, sex-crazed brutes. Simon, at all like James? Hardly. They were poles apart. Wooly anything like Gib? Bosh. Gib came closest to Aunt Fearn's stereotype of the predatory male and even Gib had displayed a noble streak. He respected strength and showed no lack of courage. He fought boldly and died with great dignity under difficult circumstances.

Gib buckled; Simon pinwheeled.

Poor Aunt Fearn. You have no inkling of the nobility of man.

CHAPTER 10

Ainsley House,
September 27, 1818

Dear Father,

As soon as James returns with help we will leave this place, surely within the next day or two. This letter will remain behind. Wooly assures me that if it is left in the right place it will reach your hands. I wonder that you don't rule the world, for your military prowess and nerves of steel amaze me. You attack without warning, shoot a man who was once a friend, and when you meet my eyes, you turn away without so much as a fare-thee-well. I am certain you recognized me. I have seen you. I know you are well. I know what you look like now, even if I have no idea what the real man is.

I shall be in Ft. William before long and, if I am very lucky, Detroit before Christmas. Only part of my goal was reached, so I leave the other part in this letter: I forgive you for leaving Mother and me. I forgive your silence across all those years. Yes, I forgive your attack on us. Indeed, Simon forgives you also; he said so. We talked quite a bit about forgiveness, Simon and I, and about fathers. Of all the things I have learned on this journey, the greatest, I think, is this: Aunt Fearn's opinion of men is without basis; she is dreadfully wrong. God bless you, Father! In spite of all, I remain your loving and faithful daughter,

Linnet

The light muslin riffled softly against her legs, then flared out as the breeze shifted. She stood at the lakeshore and watched the dimpling waters. Summer was dying before her eyes, a sad sight. Willows along the far shore were blanching in the sallow sunlight. The wall of evergreens rimming the lake had long since lost its cheery green frosting of new branchlets. Dark and somber, the trees stood waiting patiently for winter. They were made for winter, these ramrod trees.

Off to Linnet's left, cattails choked a swampy little cove. The tall stalked fruits were plump and velvety. A few were loosening, and one precocious cattail had already begun releasing its fluff into the wind. The mosquitoes had abated. The sun now peeked weakly over the spiked treetops at an odd angle; she need worry no more about freckling this year.

Far across the flat lake a loon laughed in summer's face. A sound like no other, the loon's haunting call— where did loons go when winter freezes their lake, makes their home impenetrable?

Wooly had called that snow a week ago "freak weather," too early to mean winter. But Linnet knew their warm bright days were gone. The death of summer weighed especially heavy upon Linnet this year, for more than just the summer was fading. She would not come to this country again, and her father would not leave it. She would not see him again; she could not pledge her love and forgiveness. In the larger sense, her quest had failed. Like Gib, it died not in a blaze of glory, but in a slow, painful trickle. Now she would spend weeks sitting on her bag in a canoe. She would arrive home sunburned, disheveled, nearly penniless. And her father would continue as he had for all these years, unmindful of her. Such a ragged, listless, anticlimactic end to a noble and adventuresome quest.

Linnet's eyes grew hot. She felt incredibly alone on this grassy lakeshore. She would like to sit by Simon and talk, but he was asleep. Wooly was cooking a porcupine for supper, lovingly basting it with some vile potion made from leaves. Porcupine. Honestly. Why couldn't Simon be awake and feeling better? Waddling and knowledgeable, Wooly was amusing and dependable. But Simon was all that and much, much more. He was a rock, an anchor, and she felt adrift now. She needed his solid strength. She found herself cherishing it, seeking it out.

The loon called again. No. That was no loon; it was singing. Singing! She jumped up onto a spongy, rotting stump and stood tiptoe, peering across the glassy water. She shaded her eyes, for the yellow sun angled right into them. There at the far end of the lake came a dark little spot.

She almost hopped down to fetch Wooly, but she changed her mind. His ears were sharp. He would know soon enough that someone was coming. But wait—this might be foe, not friend. No, foes were Métis and Métis rode horses. Whether North Westers or Bay people, these were friends, for her party contained ranking representatives of both companies. She listened and grinned. Those singing lusty songs in French were North Westers, come to rescue Simon

McLaren. Linnet was as good as homeward bound already.

The song changed. A smooth tenor sang some kind of verse. Between each line a robust chorus responded. Tenor, chorus, tenor, chorus—the cheer with which they sang suggested that the lyrics were too racy for polite ears.

The dark spot grew into a wedge. She could see now the smooth straight wake lines glide outward. A voice shouted and the bowman pointed toward her. The tenor sang a line, and the chorus responded, laughing. Oh, dandy! Obviously she herself was the subject of voyageur's juicy verse. She was so overjoyed she didn't care a bit.

It was a north canoe, eight yards long or more. Six men paddled, but only five wore the cheerful red stocking caps. Not only did the sixth wear a beaver hat, he was the tenor in question! James was back and singing ribald songs about her!

She jumped down off her stump as Wooly waddled by. The canoe came skimming in at full speed. At the last moment the men set their paddles. With a thunderous *whoosh!* the canoe rushed to a stop and sidled up to shore. Wooly splashed out into water thigh-deep and gripped the gunwale. He babbled in French and shook hands as everyone debarked and sloshed ashore. He even looked happy to see James. Linnet hung back, watching.

James's eyes locked on hers even before his feet hit solid ground. He jogged to her, wrapped an arm around her and pushed her at a half-trot away from the hubbub. A hundred feet from shore he turned her to him, his hands gripping her arms.

He stared intently in her eyes. "Are you all right? I was worried sick the whole time."

She smiled. "You didn't sound too sick singing your way across the lake. Just what did that one verse say about me, anyway?" She dropped the smile. He was too anxious, too humorless.

"Exactly what passed between McLaren and you while I was gone? I mean *exactly*," he demanded.

"Exactly? We talked about . . . ah . . . I don't remember exactly. Ainsley House and why it was abandoned, and the Indian troubles on the North Saskatchewan, and about fathers and forgiveness. And, ah, he asked about Detroit's . . ."

"I don't mean talk. What else?"

"What else?" She stiffened. It took her a moment to grasp his meaning. She stepped back. "You mean . . . *Mister* Landry!" She pushed his hands away. "Mr. McLaren is a gentleman and Wooly knows his place. If that's what you were worried about, for shame! You could have saved yourself a lot of fussing."

"Nothing at all? No untoward suggestions? No propositions, no advances?"

She felt her anger boiling up and she didn't want that at all. She folded her arms and cocked her head. "So you fancy that your presence here was the only restraint on his actions. My, but you think quite a bit of yourself. A true gentleman does not need another gentleman for chaperon, Mister Landry."

"Indeed." His face softened to a rather pleasant look. "One wonders, though." The face warmed to a gentle smile. He put his hands on her shoulders and she did not resist them. "Is McLaren a perfect gentleman? Or is there, shall we say, something a little bit wrong with him? A certain lack of drive? Of masculine interests? He's probably a lot older than he looks, too, you know."

"How can you say such a thing?"

He patted her shoulders. "I'm done thinking about him. Already I've forgotten any worries I might have had. Here you are, and you're even more gloriously

138

beautiful than I remember. Standing there on that stump with your skirts flowing in the breeze—ah, Linnet. Well? Say hello to the returning hero."

"Hero?"

"Two days with Mugwila. You're giggling. Believe me, a heroic effort."

"Hello, hero." Linnet initiated the kiss. She laid her hand on his neck and drew his head down to her. She reflected briefly on that first thrill of heady joy back at Cumberland House, when James proposed partnership in their quest. That joy was back again. Despite all the horrors and the boredom and the discomforts of these last few months, the joy was back again.

"If you want in on the planning, Landry, you'd best come along." Simon's voice made Linnet jump. Embarrassed, she pulled free and turned. His left arm in a fresh white sling, Simon stood on the shore path thirty feet away. He walked off toward the fallen buildings. Why should she feel so especially embarrassed that he had seen them and not anyone else?

James watched him go with loathing poorly disguised. "Let's go see what they're up to then." He wrapped his arm across her shoulders and marched briskly with her up the path. She had little time to think about much more than the savor of that kiss. Planning? Plans to return home, no doubt.

The fallen building was a brand-new place. Before it had been dark, echoing with the memory of Gib's and of Simon's suffering. Now it blazed bright with half a dozen torches, seven boisterous voices of vibrant men. The hollow cavern was crowded full with jostling bodies. Absolutely jovial, Wooly, Simon, and the five voyageurs babbled away in that slurred, rapid French. Wooly's porcupine was still cooking. The voyageurs had added their own contribution—some trout, cornbread, and hares that Linnet recognized, and a few quite mysterious side dishes.

A raucous French voice rose above the chatter. Silence. All eyes turned toward Simon. He closed his eyes and spoke in French. Linnet could discern "Thank You" and "God" amid the syllables. She recognized the "amen" clearly. Four voyageurs crossed themselves.

Wooly poked her arm. "That's how ye tell the French from the Scots."

She smiled. "So the fifth fellow there is a Britisher."

"Aye. Augie? August Swopes, Linnet MacLeod."

"Mr. Swopes." Linnet nodded to him.

"Miss MacLeod." He nodded back, then turned his attention back to his companion.

The other fellow, one of the French, wore buckskins of pale green. Linnet wondered how the fellow could possibly dye buckskin that bilious color, or why he should want to. The men started filling plates from the makeshift banquet on the hearth. They passed one of the first plates to Linnet. It was piled high with twice what she could eat. Another went to Simon, who sat on his pallet. Linnet noticed that James was expected to fill his own.

Linnet sat down close to Wooly because three others blocked her way to James or Simon. "I don't understand what's being said. They speak too fast." She tried to balance the heavy plate in her lap and still look graceful.

"Simon and I recognize the Métis who attacked us. We know who they are and where they prowl. These others are willing to go along on one more try."

"One more try for what?"

"Smoke out y'r father. Find Innis."

"No!" She barked it so loudly that everyone stopped to look at her. "We're going home. We're

140

giving up the quest. It's . . . it's . . ." She looked from face to face. "It's too late in the season now."

Simon sat cross-legged, his good elbow leaning on one knee. "If we were randomly seeking him, as we had been, it would be too late, yes. But now we know exactly where to look and we have the manpower to go after him safely. Some of these men have personal scores to settle and are more than willing. What say, Landry? Joining us?"

"I've spent the better part of a year traveling six thousand miles and more. I'm ready to spend a few more days at it."

"But . . ." She closed her mouth. She was outvoted, outnumbered. No she didn't want to go on. She was done with the whole horrible idea. Why couldn't they let it go? It wasn't their quest, it was Linnet's— Linnet's and James's. What part did these men have in it? None. But Simon said something about scores to settle. The matter was now out of her hands, beyond her power to control. She picked absently at her food and tried to sort out the foreign words these men were using.

Simon fortunately tended to articulate rather slowly when he spoke in French, just as he spoke English distinctly. He was urging them to tuck Linnet away someplace safe to wait—at some house or other or a nearby post, she imagined.

James was arguing against that. Linnet could understand some of James's French because he spoke it with a thick English accent, just as she did. He was taking her part. He insisted she deserved to be in the thick of it, having come this far. Bless dear James!

She was suddenly very weary and it was not yet dark. She wanted only to curl up on her pallet but she could not. Her bedchamber here was packed with raucous Frenchmen (and a few choice Englishmen). Absolute strangers sat on her bough bed and demonstrated for each other the latest clog steps—not elegant minuets, but awkward solo clump-clump dancing. The revelry stretched well past sundown. When Linnet was at long last able to retire, she slept fitfully. Frightening dreams in exotic settings robbed her of rest.

Gib buckled; Simon pinwheeled.

When Wooly awakened her shortly before dawn, she was just beginning to relax.

Linnet spent all that day and most of the next sitting motionless in the big north canoe. The canoe was not nearly so large as the Montreal canoes twelve yards long. But it seemed huge compared with the light canoe in which they had begun this journey.

The *avant*, the bowman, stood erect at the very front, his legs braced wide, as he casually dipped his paddle here and there. In the very stern, Wooly also stood. The idea of two men's standing safely in a canoe piqued her fancy every time she saw it. And their perfect balance and fluid movements roused her admiration.

To her left sat James. He watched the monotonous shore intently. She could not be less interested in the shore. Instead she surreptitiously watched the way his jaw muscles flexed. His face was as mobile when he was lost in thought as when he was speaking. Nothing seemed to bother him. Memories bothered Linnet.

They had left Ainsley House yesterday morning singing, as voyageurs always do. Within moments they had passed the meadow—that meadow—singing.

Gib buckled; Simon pinwheeled.

Yet a few moments more and they were portaging around LeClerc Cascade—still singing. A mile downstream, they found the shovel, and shattered parts of the light canoe. They retrieved the shovel and continued on singing. They sang the day away. And now this morning they had set out singing as bravely as ever.

All morning they sang as they threaded an intricate maze of streams and riffles. They laughed amid their song as they bounded up rapids. Twice, the middle men—*les milieus*—hopped out into the rushing stream to lighten the canoe and ease it across giggling riffles.

Even Wooly joined their songs. Linnet had heard that a voyageur was chosen partly on the basis of his singing voice. Hearing him now, she was fairly certain Wooly had worked his way up through the ranks. He would never have passed muster as a singer.

James, too, joined some of the songs; his repertoire was growing. Simon sat silent.

Sometime in midafternoon, Simon spoke for the first time. *"Cela suffit. Retournez, s'il vous plait."*

Enough? What was enough? And where were they returning? Linnet twisted carefully to look at Simon. His eyes met hers briefly and flicked away shoreward.

The bowman set his paddle deep and wedged outward. The canoe swung about. It wavered slightly in the current and headed back downstream.

Moments ago they sang lustily. They paddled silently, grimly now. The quiet hung so heavy that Linnet could hear Simon's labored breathing behind her. Was their travel too arduous for him? Or was the anticipation of danger shortening his breath? He had abandoned the white sling. Whether sitting or walking, he simply kept his thumb hooked in his belt. He still could not use his left arm at all.

The current ran strong here, much faster than Linnet would have guessed from looking at the flat river. Wending upstream they had been paddling strongly and making moderate speed. Now, moving with the current, they glided swiftly between the dark green walls. *Pour le pais sauvage!* the voyageurs were

fond to cry: "For the wild land, the savage land."
Savage? It seemed so peaceful, this land. Asleep.
Dark and glassy, the river coursed noiselessly through
the midst of the silent forest. The *milieus* shipped
their paddles; only Wooly and the bowman directed
their course.

"*Voila*," the bowman whispered. He waved off to
the left. Wooly was already directing the canoe
toward some chosen spot along the bank.

"*Bon*," Simon whispered. "*Pret, Messieurs?*"

Even before the canoe bobbed to a rocking halt in a
little backwater, the man in green buckskins had
jumped out and splashed into water waist-high (and a
very quiet splash it was for a man so stocky). He
reached behind as the water splashed again beside
Linnet's ear. Simon was struggling in the water beside
her. He was waving his pistol high in his good right
hand, trying to keep the powder dry. The other fellow
grabbed his arm, steadied him, and together they
waded ashore. They disappeared dripping among the
somber, silent trees.

A sudden cold, hard fear seized Linnet's heart and
pushed it high into her throat. Her protector had just
abandoned her. No matter that she sat in a canoe full
of able men, one of whom was obviously attracted to
her romantically. No matter that Simon was practically an invalid, crippled and easily worn down. No
matter that hale and hearty James could tackle
anything. She took a long, deep breath. How foolish!
Her mind played such impish tricks on her.

They sat in the silence, bobbing, waiting. After an
eternity Wooly whispered "Now, lads." The canoe
backed up ten feet and nosed into the current. They
pressed close to shore, barely beyond reach of the
clawing overhanging branches. The river swung out to
the right into a broad, casual meander. They followed

the sweeping gooseneck and drifted. Only Wooly's paddle touched water.

The wall on the left opened somewhat into a tree-studded park. A light canoe had been dragged up on the bank, half ashore and half awash. Its tail bobbed in the wind ripples; its nose nodded counterpoint. With scarcely any movement at all, Wooly checked the canoe's speed. They hovered hard beside the shore-bound forest. Moments dragged like hours.

Linnet reflected that this was indeed much like a fox hunt. Instead of large and powerful horses, the hunters were riding a large and powerful canoe. The hounds were Simon and James and Wooly who, having caught the scent, would not let it go. The huntsmen, these voyageurs, eagerly followed the hounds, and Linnet was one of them. Her quest had become *la chasse*, and her father might well be at bay. The huntsmen were clever. They knew they could not come upstream unawares, so they passed their quarry noisily. And now they had returned, hot on the trail. That icicle of fear chilled her breastbone again.

Linnet heard rustling among the trees. Simon? No. Two men in red leggings popped out into the open park. Each carried a canoe paddle. Linnet clapped her hands over her mouth. She craned out around James to get her first truly good look at her father. His beard was indeed the color of her own hair, almost exactly. He was stoutly built and perhaps a wee bit shorter than Simon. He moved like a cat; he flowed like liquid across the grassy park. He carried that long ugly rifle, cradled lovingly at his side. Was the gun a part of him, an extension of the man Innis MacLeod? The two men tossed their paddles into their canoe and gave it a shove. It scooted backward off the grass and floated free.

Linnet's north canoe surged forward. The heads of the two men snapped up; they gaped in unison. The *milieus'* paddles braked against swirling water. Her craft wagged in place, blocking the way of the light canoe.

Linnet's father shouted something in Cree. Wild-eyed, his companion shook his head. The Métis glanced at the canoe where Linnet sat transfixed, glanced behind, glanced to either side—then raced headlong for the forest. Linnet's father stood a long, long moment, teetering on the razor edge of indecision.

"George's whiskers, we got him!" James breathed. He seemed absolutely amazed that their plan—whatever it was—should work. His hand darted to the pistol in his belt. He yanked it free and swung it toward Linnet's father.

Linnet yelped. "No! Don't!" Without thinking she lunged across James's lap and grabbed for his wrist. Her weight carried his arm down *clunk!* against the gunwale. The pistol blammed; dirty gray smoke obscured her vision and burned her nostrils. The canoe sloshed recklessly to their left. The *milieus* and Wooly shouted. The canoe rolled just as wildly to the right. Icy wetness stabbed through her clothes and soaked her—water over the gunwales or water from a split seam. Either way, she was causing chaos.

James didn't help the canoe a bit. He was struggling with her, trying to disentangle her from his wrist and lap. She heard her father's buffalo gun roar.

Gib buckled; Simon pinwheeled.

Why was she risking so much in defense of that murderous old reprobate? Because he was her father, that was why! She tried to extricate herself from the tangle and could not. The canoe wallowed drunkenly.

Wooly's voice cried, "Ashore, lads! *A terre! A terre!*"

Another gun fired from somewhere up among the trees.

Linnet got one hand on solid wood to push herself erect. She could see the gunwale in front of her nose. She raised her eyes—and stared into her father's eyes! He was right here, right at their canoe. From nowhere a gaudy paddle came whistling down and just missed his head. It splashed in the water beside his ear.

"Y'r a good lass!" her father grinned. His dripping hands were both on the gunwale. He was pulling them over, dragging them atilt. The canoe tipped toward him, down, down . . . His own head disappeared beneath the water as the canoe slipped gracefully out from under James and Linnet and everybody.

Instantly Linnet was buried in a cold river full of thrashing arms and legs. Even as she herself thrashed, the back of her mind told her that none of these wild limbs was her father's. He was no doubt hauling himself into his own canoe now, paddling away to safety.

The fox had won. Again.

CHAPTER 11

> By a streamside
> who-knows-where,
> September 30, 1818

Dear Aunt Fearn,

What a mess! Just as I thought things could get no worse, they did. I don't know how Simon (Mr. McLaren) managed to do it, but earlier this afternoon he singled out your brother from among the group of half-breeds who are his companions. It seemed for a moment that our quest was over. Then an unfortunate chain of events prevented our actual contact. The best I can say at this juncture is that your brother is healthy and in fine spirits. The last I saw of him, he was grinning.

One of the items in the aforementioned chain was a ducking. You can well imagine these round-bottomed canoes tip easily. We all escaped the tipover unharmed, but Messrs. MacPherson and McLaren were delayed in their pursuit of your brother because they had to help me ashore—you are aware I cannot swim.

*Fortunately another of our party was on shore and he
hurried off to retrieve our canoe, which was bound
downstream upside down, on its own. Now Mr.
Landry is intensely angry with me. He claims I caused
the whole mishap by misreading his intentions completely. Mr. MacPherson is philosophical. These
voyageur French canoemen simply laugh and sing
throughout it all. They really don't care a bit whether
they are wet or dry. And Mr. McLaren acts bemused.
He can afford to; he was wetted only to the thighs.
Indeed, I believe he is quietly reveling in Mr. Landry's
discomfiture.*

*Now here I sit shivering, all goose-bumps, in the
white muslin dress while my woolen dress dries beside
the fire.*

Linnet laid aside her writing materials and knelt
closer to the fire. She rubbed her hands together; her
fingers were nearly too stiff to write. One of the
Frenchmen, ever gallant, put some thick dry sticks on
the fire. It crackled, stuttered, and flared high,
shooting sparks.

James paced back and forth on the far side of the
fire. He stared a moment at two voyageurs who were
muttering in animated conversation over by a rock-
pile. He looked at the man in green buckskins. "Why
are we sitting here doing nothing while that brigand is
putting miles and more miles between himself and
us?"

The Frenchmen shrugged and smiled disarmingly.

James's eyes flitted past Linnet as if she didn't exist
and settled on Mr. Swopes. "Why are we just sitting
here, Swopes?"

"Enjoying the last fair evening we'll see for a time,
I vow. Relax y'rself."

Wooly popped out of the trees and squatted by the
fire to pour himself a mug of tea.

James descended on him with arms flying. "Why

aren't we doing something, MacPherson? And where's McLaren, anyway?"

"Coming, lad. He's coming." Wooly sipped at the scalding brown scum.

James opened his mouth and closed it again, disgusted. That curl dropped down across his forehead. Why did that one errant lock have such an hypnotic effect on Linnet? She enjoyed watching him, angry or not.

Simon came rambling out from the trees. He was looking a little pale again. He sat down on a rock and Wooly passed him a mug of tea. He dropped forward to his favorite slouch, his elbows on his knees. "Have a cup of tea, Mr. Landry." Simon stared into his own mug. "Drink it fast, though, before it rots the cup."

"Where have you been?" James paused by Simon's ear.

"That rocky little ridge above us there, looking at the sky."

"We won't find MacLeod in the sky." James smiled briefly, pleased with his own pun. He was now the only person standing. He perched on a rock beside Simon's, probably to get eye-level with the rest of the world.

Simon gestured toward the others. "These men have as much experience as I at reading weather, perhaps more. I invite their comment, but Wooly and I think we've seen the last of the sun for this year. For some reason winter has her claws out early. Animal sign all over: the moose are yarding up in the low valleys already. Bears are digging in. The muskrats have enough grass stockpiled to last through three winters. The birds are gone. And when the sky takes on that leaden sheen like a newly-poured bullet, it intends to stay murky for a while."

"You're saying we're likely to get snowed in up here? Stranded here in the hinterland until melt-out?"

"Oh, we'd make it out eventually, overland. But we

150

don't have dogs, so it would be slow going. And very difficult for Linnet here. She's held up well so far, but slogging through woods in the dead of winter is something else again."

James glanced at her without seeing her. "But we have time to canoe out."

"I think we can raise Fort William. If we get there before the last express canoe leaves, we might even reach Montreal. But we'll have to be very fortunate—and paddle like ducks."

"Montreal may be your hang-out, but it's not mine. Straight downriver to York Factory. Twenty days maximum."

"You can't outrun winter by traveling north, Landry. York will snow shut six weeks before Montreal feels the pinch. You've seen York Factory. I wager you'll be far better pleased with the amenities in Montreal if we can just get there."

"If! And if not, I sit in the North Westers' nest for five months."

"Better than this whole crew sitting in a Hudson's Bay fort unprofitably. However,"—Simon sat e-rect—"Wooly and I think we just might make it to Montreal. We'll have to hit the ground running in the morning; packed up and on the water before dawn."

Mr. Swopes was nodding sagely.

"And MacLeod goes his merry way, the victor in this hunt." James sagged forward and propped his chin in his hands. "Blazes," His face was the picture of dejection. "We had him. We were so close. Now he's so far away."

Simon glanced at James with that bemused twinkle. "As I know Innis MacLeod, the old fox is perched in some treetop within a mile of us, watching and gloating."

James raised his head to stare at Simon. "Surely he's not that big a fool!"

"Fool? Hardly. He knows we must leave without

him. He can read the weather as well as any of us."
With a great tip-up, Simon drained his cup.

James rubbed his face with both hands. "The crowning insult. The final indignity. To wave good-by to our departing backs."

Linnet thought about Simon's words. Was he simply baiting James, or did he speak the truth? Might her father really be watching from somewhere close by? Simon had called him a fox. Had he indeed doubled back to spy on his pursuers? If so, he could see best from uphill of this camp. Linnet waited a few more minutes, then casually stood up, stretched, and sauntered past the men who were absorbed in their conjecturing.

Once beyond sight of the fire ring and the posted lookout, Linnet walked faster. She followed a faint deer trail until it disappeared completely. Beyond the trees ahead and to the left, she could hear a fall or steep cascade of some sort. The howling water was unmistakable, even though she could see very little through the dense tangle of trunks and limbs. She climbed a ragged, rocky hillside and paused in the middle of a pleasant little glade, enjoying the openness of this grassy meadow; the forest crowded so close so constantly.

With the distance between herself and camp, plus the roar of the cascade, she was surely beyond earshot of her companions. She called out, "Father?" She repeated it, louder this time. "Faa-therr!"

A breeze ruffled the treetops and whispered through dead grass at her feet. The cascade's crashing thunder made a curtain of noise beyond the forest. Yet the meadow rang with silence.

She took a deep breath. "Father! Innis MacLeod! I am Linnet, your daughter!"

Suddenly she flushed with embarrassment. She had taken Simon's word for something ridiculous, and now here she stood making an utter fool of herself.

Simon was leading James on and she fell for it! Where could her wits have flown to? Now she would be hard-pressed to make it back to camp and safety before dark. What if she got lost in these thick woods? What if . . . She turned around to start back and froze in place.

Innis MacLeod stood at the edge of the clearing not five yards away, intently watching his daughter. With one leg cocked, he leaned casually on the muzzle of his long, upended buffalo gun.

Mindlessly she walked to him through the broken grass. She looked into that face, so like her own in many ways. She had rehearsed her speech countless times. Why did the words flee now? She wanted to tell him she loved him in spite of all. She wanted to tell him she forgave him for never being a father to her, for never being a husband to her poor, star-crossed mother. She wanted to tell him how happy she was to meet him at last. She would be the perfect daughter, awash in grace, whether he deserved such a jewel or not.

Gib buckled; Simon pinwheeled.

"Ye still live in Detroit, lass?"

She nodded numbly.

"Fearn still herself?"

She bobbed her head.

He wagged his head grinning. "Bet the old witch still knows how to frazzle a man. That voice a-nagging, that finger wiggling in y'r face . . ."

"She's a noble woman who accepted a responsibility that was never hers, and at great personal sacrifice. I could have grown up in a foundling home or died in some alley—all the same to you, whose responsibility I was. She raised me, she educated me, and she taught me how to support myself with honest work. Don't you dare ever say another demeaning word about her."

"Eh, ye got a point there, I aver. A point."

Gib buckled.

"I wanted . . . I wish . . . ah . . . I don't . . . ah . . . Why did you do it?"

Simon pinwheeled

"Do it, lass?"

"Leave her. She was a pretty woman, a good woman. Would it have been so horrible to fulfill your vows to her? Were we such a burden?" Her voice was rising and she could not lower it. It was beyond her control. She laid both hands on her chest. "I have a father-shaped hole here and you're the only one who could have filled it. I'm not complete. I . . ." *Gib buckled.* "lack, and you could have eased the lack— with a visit, with a letter, with a kind word—" *Simon pinwheeled.* "anything to make you real."

"I sent drafts. Didn't they reach ye?"

"Drafts! Where was your face, your voice, your touch? I needed *you!*" She was shouting now, strident. She didn't want this at all. She wanted to forgive him, speaking softly.

"I wish I could undo what's done and make some of it up to ye, lass."

"Undo? Gib died slowly and painfully. Gutshot. You know Gib—striped vest. They buried him folded up, the way he died, so they wouldn't have to dig as much. And Simon . . ."

"Simon? Eh," he nodded, "I thought that might be McLaren, though things were happening so fast I wasn't sure. He's got glasses since I knew him. Probably because of what that big Canuck did to his eye. DuBois. Dalles DuBois."

"You thought you recognized him. Did you know me?"

"Aye, lass. The word I heard was that ye were an imposter—bait for a trap. But when I saw ye, I knew ye. That angel face—the shapely figger—all y'r mother's. And the way ye . . ." He stopped. His eyes bulged wide. He was looking not at Linnet but beyond

154

her. His arm whipped out and knocked her into the crisp brown grass. He swung his rifle waist-high. His finger on the trigger, he leveled it on . . .

Simon! He was standing silently at the far side of the glade. He took a step forward and stopped. Linnet twisted around to her knees.

Innis side-stepped, putting Linnet between himself and Simon. He called, "We worked together once. We even kissed the same girls. And y've turned on me, ye red-backed traitor. Consorting with Bay people yet! So use that pistol in y'r belt there, McLaren. Make an end to the matter, and I'll take ye with me."

"And risk Linnet to a stray slug? No. And I trust you won't, either. Why Seven Oaks, Innis? Why innocent settlers?"

"Innocent? Bay people, ye blind fool! They might've had a separate charter, and they might've answered to the home secretary, but they were Bay people. You and Ellis, and McGillivray—the agents—the partners—ye were all afraid to step out and do. Robertson, he's doing for the Bay company, but all ye could think of was to write letters. Bah! Ye sat back and watched 'em dig in. So I acted. I did it for the company because the company's too cowardly to do it for itself."

"Rivalry is one thing, Innis. But murder? You're responsible for over two dozen deaths that I know of, and that doesn't include Indians. I'm not consorting with Bay boys. I'm here on my own. The only way I know to end your slaughter is to stop you here and now."

"So ye turn my own flesh and blood against me." Innis reached forward with a moccasined foot and jabbed a toe at Linnet. "And y'rself, ye witch! Leading him here to me. Betrayed by my friends, by my own company, and now by my own daughter."

"No! I didn't! Simon, tell him!" She swung around

to Simon. She gasped as the truth struck her so forcibly the breath was forced from her body. "*That's* why you said what you said to James! You knew I'd come looking for him if I thought he might be near. You used me! How could you . . . ?"

Simon ignored her, his eyes never leaving Innis's face for a moment. He came walking out through the scratchy weeds, catlike. His stride was firm and measured. His arms swung loosely at his sides. There was no hint, absolutely no hint, of the injury that had so recently laid him low. Innis MacLeod would see nothing to suggest that Simon's fighting power had at all diminished. He even appeared invincible to Linnet and she knew better.

Innis's buffalo gun ticked ominously. He had thumbed the flintlock back.

"No. Both of you! No!" Linnet's helplessness frustrated her. Why couldn't she say what she wanted to say? Why could she do nothing about this?

"She's all you have left, Innis." Simon's voice rumbled. "Be careful around her."

"I know how ye work, Simon. MacPherson's somewhere out in the trees with that rusty old squirrel gun of his. But I say as long as you're in front of my muzzle, he won't pull his trigger." He raised his voice. "Hear that, Wooly? I know y're there!" He waggled his gun at Simon. "Stop! Stay back or I'll show ye whether I'm worried about Wooly. Now either y've turned traitor and y'r Bay people now, or y'll let y'r old trapping buddy go."

"So you can kill again? No. I may die by your hand today, but I guarantee I'll take you with me. It's over, Innis." Simon's eyes flicked briefly off toward the trees beyond her father. A shadow, a slight, puckered frown, flashed across his face so quickly Linnet wasn't sure she saw it. She looked up at her father. Did he see it?

He did. He started backing up, angling away,

moving toward the trees. Simon swung wide as he came; Linnet was no longer directly between them. Linnet tried to pick out Wooly among the trees. The forest looked exactly alike, all of it. The trees stood harmless in the waning light of evening.

Simon was beside her now. His strong right arm pressed her into the coarse weeds. "Stay flat. Hear me?"

Innis spun on his heel and bolted away, crashing through the grass and brush. Simon yanked the pistol from his belt and lurched into a staggering run.

Stay down? She couldn't! Linnet sprang to her feet and ran after them.

Somewhere up ahead, the buffalo gun blasted. It was spent now. Useless. The pistol fired. What was happening up there? She gathered her skirts high and ran faster. She stumbled over weeds and dead branches. She clawed through barren head-high bushes and crowds of sapling trees. That waterfall was directly ahead now. Her ear could pick out the crash of a constant cascade as well as the hollow roll of free-falling water. It pounded her ears; she could hear nothing else.

Where were they? And where was Wooly? Their guns were both spent but Wooly's was not. He should be behind her or beside her. Or was Wooly nearby at all?

She saw Simon away ahead, flitting among the tangled trees like an agile doe. One stride took him up on a fallen log; he pushed off flying and disappeared beyond.

Linnet's hem caught on a branch and stopped her cold. She yanked her skirt fiercely; the fabric ripped. She ran to the log. It was too high to jump or to cross as Simon had done. She scrambled onto it. The loose, mossy bark gave way; her grip failed and she slipped back.

They were flailing in the brush beyond, a single

prostrate tangle of arms and legs. One of them grunted, a painful sound. They rolled apart. Innis bolted to his feet, staggered, fell, and rose again. He ran off virtually on one leg; the other was bloodied from top to ankle.

Simon jerked himself up to his knees, swaying a moment. Gripping his middle, he struggled to his feet and took off in pursuit.

Linnet leaped onto the log and literally fell off the other side (a remarkably easy thing to do). She scrambled to her feet and ran after them. She was no woodsman, but even she could follow the splashes of bright red blood—her father's blood. The waterfall was deafening now.

Up ahead on a shining wet rock, her father stood facing her. He propped on his one good leg and balanced a big skinning knife in his hand. He was shouting something she could not make out. Less than a yard behind him the world fell away into a foggy chasm. Beyond his heels howling water plunged, wild and jubilant, into the deep canyon. What should have been a vast and empty crack in the world was instead filled with mist and danger and hellish noise.

Simon crouched facing Innis, his own knife in his good right hand. Her father must feel trapped with the canyon behind him and his erstwhile friend before him. Linnet was close enough now to hear what they were saying.

Innis waved hand and arm at Linnet. He screamed above the water's noise, "Ye brought me to ruin, ye little vixen! I trust y'r vengeance is satisfied sufficiently now."

No! No, no, no! That wasn't it at all! Bereft of words, Linnet could only shake her head and stammer. How could he think such a thing of his own daughter? That wasn't it at all! No!

Simon said something.

Innis wagged his head. "Ye've shown y'r true

colors, Simon. Ye should've shot to kill. Finish the matter."

"You're not condemned, Innis." Simon's voice was strong, smooth, resonant—a warm contrast to the discordant howl beyond.

"She said Gib died."

"But you didn't pull that trigger. Gib was down when you fired at me, remember? And I'm not about to accuse you."

"Accuse? Yerself calls me a killer, and that's the general opinion, I aver. Don't try to sweet-talk me, Simon. I know y'r glib tongue." Innis looked at Linnet. "Aren't there any murderers in Wayne County, that ye must come clear up here to look at one?"

She wagged her head, distraught. "You're not a murderer. You're my fa—"

He laughed; it was a wicked cackle, full of glee. "No? Simon's pegged it right. Farmers and women and children by the score." His eyes danced between Simon and Linnet, watching them both. "If I could start over, I'd have a happy wife and daughter and how many other kids, eh? I wouldn't be hounded by Bay boys or my own false friends. I'd be different. But ye can't start over."

Linnet grabbed Simon's arm. "You accepted Gib's change of heart. Now let my father go! Quickly, before Wooly and the others get here!"

"I can't do that." He gripped her sleeve and pulled her around behind him, out of harm's way. She couldn't even see her father.

She broke loose; it wasn't hard, struggling against his injured side. She ducked back out to face her father. "Then give up, Father, please. Perhaps we can have a few days together before you . . . before they . . . I don't want you to go . . . to leave again without . . . ." She was stammering again.

"A few days more of talking, eh? So ye can tell me some more what a rotten pig I am. How much I did ye

159

wrong. But ye ignore all them drafts. Sometimes they were half what I made in a year. Good hefty work went into them drafts. Wading in frozen beaver ponds, riding for days after buffalo, Shivering cold and going hungry. I did the best I could for ye, for what I am. I gave ye the best I had. So I fell short of what ye want, eh? I trust this'll even the score between us. I can see the end when it's right before me." He wheeled around and paused on the lip of the world.

Linnet shrieked. Simon lunged forward with both hands, grabbing.

Innis MacLeod tipped forward casually, smoothly. Instantly he was sucked down into the swirling fog. Linnet fell face forward on the shining rock. She dragged herself to the brink to see. The crashing water had swallowed him.

The world stopped. The waters froze in midleap. Her scream hung forever amid the crowd of noise. She gripped the cold, wet rock; she wanted to go, too. A warm hand grasped her arm and dragged her back, breaking her gaze, tearing her eyes away from the thunder below. She was being gathered in close against that black wool coat. She struggled.

Suddenly her mind snapped clear. Her ears pounded, yet she wasn't hysterical anymore. She wasn't even distraught. Tears coursed down her face, but she wasn't crying. With perfect clarity she saw it all. And she was angry—as intensely, satisfyingly, completely enraged as she had ever been in her life.

She pushed away to meet Simon face to face, eye to eye. "You accepted Gib's change of heart freely. But you wouldn't accept my father's. If you had . . ."

"I've known him for twenty years, Linnet. He didn't mean it. He was saying whatever he thought would manipulate us best."

"You didn't accept his change of heart! He changed and you wouldn't believe him! You tricked me into drawing him out, with what you said to James. And then you . . ."

"No, I didn't. I saw you go and followed, afraid you'd get lost. It wasn't until you were halfway up the hill that I real . . ."

"You deliberately *used* me! You poisoned him against me and said nothing in my defense. You let him die hating me. He died needlessly"

"He didn't hate you. He was . . ."

"He died needlessly because you wouldn't let him do anything else! You think you're God, that you can send a man to his death because you think he deserves it?"

"Linnet, if I had wanted him to die, I'd have killed him outright with that pistol ball. I didn't want him dead. You don't understand. You don't know him. He's a conniver. You don't know how he can . . ."

"No! No, I don't know him. And now I never will, because you just took away my last and only chance to know him." Her breath was coming in wild sobs now. "He died hating me. He died to spite me, because of you. You robbed me of everything. Simon McLaren, I hate you as purely as a person can hate another. And I will loathe you until the day I die."

CHAPTER 12

Montreal, December 15, 1818

Dear Aunt Fearn,

I have had several opportunities to write to you, but until now I have not been able to collect my thoughts adequately to do so. My father died on the thirtieth day of September. I am very sorry. I shall relate the exact circumstances of his death when I return to Detroit. That will be as soon as the lake ice breaks up and ships resume movement. I have no idea exactly where he died, but the North West Company here in Montreal must have maps of the region. I will try to find out before spring.

The last two months have been a nightmare, and I myself feel like a sleepwalker. After my father's death our party traveled in haste to Fort William. Neither Mr. Landry nor myself wished to be trapped in the interior by winter snows. No one was coming south to Detroit, my desired destination. Then Simon McLaren conjured up a freight canoe bound for Montreal here (a freight canoe is intermediate in size between the north canoe and the great Montreal canoe; it carries no freight other than its own provisions and its purpose is speed, the swift transfer of personnel and messages). Mr Landry and I both purchased passage, eager to be quit of Fort William and all its ghosts of the past, for my father spent many winters there. Simon did not accompany us. No sooner did he arrange our way for us than he disappeared back into the hinterland. He tarried only long enough to put in an earnest petition to me concerning God.

I have never been one to enjoy preaching, but preaching from him? Hardly! That man, Aunt Fearn, was the primary instrument in your brother's death. I told him bluntly that I would not give an ear to his pleadings about God or Jesus Christ.

For a while I discounted your wisdom regarding men; I see now how very right you are. I quickly became disenchanted with James Landry, the way he huffed and snorted all over Fort William. He acted as if he had been robbed of some splendid trophy to carry off to England. My father, a trophy! Indeed. And the notion that he might be stranded amongst North Westers put his temper completely out of sorts, so that he was singularly unpleasant to be around. I became so angry with his petulance that I refused to humble myself with words of forgiveness (What had I to forgive? It wasn't really my fault that canoe tipped over) nor did I court his company. We both sulked all the way to Montreal.

Here, though, I have obtained a very pleasant position as maid in the home of a wealthy fur dealer. The lady of the house is a cheerful sort who seeks only to serve her husband. He in turn devotes himself tenderly to her. Their children are grown, but they will return to visit over the Christmas holidays. Mr. Higgins is an exemplary father—jovial yet authoritative. A curious turn, this, for I have been thinking long and deeply about fathers—what they are and what is expected of them.

You would enjoy Montreal, I think. It is quite European and very elegant. Again, I am truly sorry about your brother. I am

> *your dutiful niece,*
> *Linnet*

Linnet hitched up her skirts and bounded down the staircase two-steps-at-a-time. She jogged the length of the hall and reached the big front door on the second knock. When she pulled the door open a gust of frozen air whipped in, all dotted with snowflakes. An impeccably dressed young man, hardly more than a boy, followed the swirl inside. Linnet slammed the door shut against the wind.

The young man sighed heavily and pulled off his beaver hat. "Messenger service. This the Hector Higgins residence?"

"Yes, but the master is out for the day, as is the lady. They should be back by dark."

"The message is for a Linnet MacLeod—supposed to be at this address."

She cocked her head. "Who would . . . ? I mean . . . from whom?"

"I just deliver it. You're Linnet MacLeod?"

"Yes. Aunt Fearn perhaps. But she couldn't possibly . . ." Linnet stood perplexed as the young man pressed a large foolscap envelope into her hand. Belatedly she remembered her manners and duty. She pointed off toward the kitchen. "That way. The cook, Marisetta, will warm you up with tea and scones."

"Thanks, Mum, I'm supposed to wait for your answer." He bobbed his head and trotted off toward the warm kitchen.

With both Higginses absent, Linnet had the parlor

to herself. She settled into the big wingback chair by the window and carefully cracked the wax seal. She opened the envelope and unfolded the letter carefully, in no hurry.

My dear Linnet,

I discovered just recently where you are staying. Three items of business; The first: I offer my condolences upon the death of your father. I overheard you say at Fort William that you felt no social obligation to go into mourning for a father you never really had, but the man's death must have been a blow to you all the same. Secondly: I apologize for my short temper. It was inexcusable. Thirdly: I wish to make amends for my churlish behavior toward such a charming partner-in-questing. I have in hand an invitation to a ball this Christmas Eve. I escorted you in questing. Now may I also escort you to the ball? Each region and city has its peculiarities as regards the lively arts, dancing foremost. For that reason a dancing master will call at your door tomorrow morning, Tuesday, December 22. He will instruct you in the dance as it is performed here in Montreal. Again, my deepest condolences.

> Ever your servant,
> James

Linnet read it through again, just to make sure it said what she thought it said. Dear James. Dear, sweet James! He knew she had absolutely no experience dancing at a ball. Never in Detroit had she been escorted to any social event of that sort. How tactfully he handled the matter. And how thoughtful he was to think of a dancing instructor in the first place. Of course, were he to escort her to the ball, as ignorant as she was, he, too, would look the fool as she fumbled and erred. Her instruction was as much for his benefit as hers. Still . . . he did ask her!

She couldn't go; there was no question about that. She had only that torn white muslin dress, the frumpy woolen dress, and this maid's dress, black with white lace cuffs. She could not possibly contract a dressmaker in time to finish a gown in three days, not even if she located the fastest dressmaker in Montreal this very minute. And with what would she pay a dressmaker?

Besides, this affair was clearly high society. Linnet had no pretensions, though James fit right in. She was a cleaning lady and a maid. No more. Her country manners would only embarrass him. Yet, Aunt Fearn had schooled her thoroughly in proper behavior.

Besides else, the Higginses would need her service on Christmas Eve. They would surely be receiving callers. Their children and grandchildren would fill the house. Marisetta couldn't handle it all. No, all things considered, she must refuse his generous invitation.

Linnet stood up and paused beside the window. For the moment she fancied herself the mistress of this great house. She looked out her plate glass window at the swirling snow. She rested her hand on the arm of her chair, and ran her fingers down its rich brocade upholstery. Mistress of the house. She strolled across the Turkish carpet to the slim little writing table by the south window. She sat down in its padded mahogany chair. She chose a sheet of stationery from the pigeonhole on the far left and opened the ink. She tapped the pen to her tongue, considered a moment, then dipped the nib into the ink pot. Her hand hesitated hardly at all as she wrote her brief reply for the messenger to take back to James.

My dear James,

Your apology, your condolences and your invitation—I accept all with thanks, in great humility. I will expect the arrival tomorrow morning of the instructor you mentioned. I look forward greatly to your charming company. Thank you again!

Your partner in questing,
Linnet

She waved the ink dry, for she didn't want to use Mrs. Higgins's sand. She folded the note with exaggerated care. She took it and the sealing wax to the kitchen, for there was no candle lighted here in the parlor. In moments the boy was on his way and there she stood.

Now look what she had done! The things she wanted to do she did not. The things she ought not to do she did. She would never have pictured herself as such a perverse and fickle person. There wasn't a way in the world she could go to that ball, and now she would ruin James's evening as well. She returned the sealing wax to its place with her mind in a fog.

The front door roared open and in came Mrs. Higgins. Her mind still elsewhere, Linnet took the cape and hat, hung them carefully, and followed her mistress upstairs. Mrs. Higgins hustled to her bedroom and began pawing through her clothes press.

"Mister Higgins should be home before dark. I'll dress now for dinner." The lady studied her gray dress, her brown one, her blue one. "This one tonight, I believe." She yanked one from the wardrobe; Linnet didn't notice which.

Linnet helped the portly lady change. She plumped the puff sleeves. She arranged the lady's gray-brown hair. And except for a short thought as she compared Mrs. Higgins's soft round pudginess with Mugwila's iron-hard pudginess, she pondered that accursed invitation. Why, oh, why had she said such a thing?!

"Young lady, step around here and look at me!" Mrs. Higgins twisted on her vanity stool. Her dense torso flexed only slightly, so she craned her head. "Now what's going on here? You've not said a word,

167

even when spoken to. And you've certainly not heard a word *I've* said."

Linnet clamped her teeth over her lower lip a moment. "Ah, well . . . ah . . ." She sighed. "I've got myself into a pickle, Mum."

The gentle eyes widened in horror. "Oh, no! A nice girl like you? I would never suspect—I mean . . ."

"Oh, no, Mum! Not *that* sort of a pickle. A social matter. You see, a gentleman—and I assure you he is a gentleman—has invited me to some sort of Christmas Eve ball. And with my foolish head in a cloud, I accepted. Now, of course, I must undo my foolishness and I don't even know where he's staying. I must reverse my acceptance."

"The ball. My, my. Is he a gentleman of breeding?"

"Yes'm, a Londoner. An officer in H- . . . ah, some sort of fur company. I met him at Cumberland House this last summer."

"And why can't you go?"

"You need me. And, ah, he wouldn't want to escort a woman dressed like a maid, surely. And I'm not of that social station, Mum. And, ah . . ."

"Bosh. All bosh. You've bleached out considerably since you arrived; those freckles don't show as much any more. Your face has a more pleasant tone, and your hair is just lovely. You have a natural grace and you've been trained well." Mrs. Higgins marched across the room. "You'll pass muster, Linnet. Don't give it a second thought."

"But, Mum! I . . . ah . . . I mean . . ."

Mrs. Higgins was pushing around in her clothes press again. "This was my daughter's. She outgrew it—in girth, I mean—when she started making me a grandmother. I've been planning to take it to Barbara and have it made over, but I never got to it. Barbara's a splendid dressmaker. Your aunt taught you to sew, did she not?"

"Yes'm, but plain stitchery—I've never sewn anything fancy like . . ." Her words stopped coming. The gown was lovely, even if a bit dated. Mrs. Higgins held it out at arm's length, studying it critically. If the waistline were raised and the neckline altered; remove the heavy gathered overskirt and reset the pleats farther back . . .

Mrs. Higgins wadded the dress into Linnet's hands. "You'll have snatches of time here and there. Surely you can alter it in time for the ball. You shall attend, Linnet, with our blessing. It's a glorious occasion, the best of the season. Every girl should attend once in her lifetime, and it would seem this is your year." Mrs. Higgins waved a chubby arm. "Now let's not just stand about. I hear the front door. That will be the Mister. Hurry me here, dear. I must finish up and get downstairs."

For the next two days Linnet sewed on her gown at every spare moment. And she daydreamed. What did she dream about? If Aunt Fearn could read her mind now, the poor lady would turn purple and drop over! Linnet thought of James—his touch, his kiss, his handsome smile.

And in spite of herself she found herself thinking about Simon. They were not thoughts of immorality, although she remembered fondly the peaceful comfort she felt when he held her. When compared with James, he was not at all dazzling, even say dull. Yet he was dull—if that were the word—by choice. She was sure from a variety of sources that he had once been wild and profligate. The very first time they met, he mentioned something about fathering bastard children in the woods somewhere. Either he had been changed, or he had changed himself—or both. And he seemed content with the change.

She thought of the arduous journey from Fort William to Montreal. There were long stretches of it

169

she could not remember at all. Her memory stored only fragments: James's sulking and snapping. Had James not been so out of sorts and wearied, might he have pursued the romantic aspect of their partnership? Perhaps she was too numb to recognize his overtures. And now that she thought about it, she did not remember any occasion when she and James were alone. One of Simon's men hovered near her almost constantly the whole trip.

Simon . . . Simon . . . Simon. Every time she wanted something, or sought something or needed something, there was Simon. He might hinder or he might help, but he somehow always had a finger in the pie. She felt just a wee bit guilty about rebuffing him so firmly. But Simon was past. For better or worse, she had ended all contact with him.

The future was James.

CHAPTER 13

Montreal, December 24, 1818

Dear Aunt Fearn,

It has occurred to me that all these letters may arrive at your door at the same time—spring break-up. It is evening and I am awaiting James's carriage. I am writing now because I am too excited to just sit; yet I must sit and wait. The Higginses excused me from service this evening, and Mr. Higgins is making much humor in the fact that my head has not been together all day. Mrs. Higgins loaned a gown which I remade, and it turned out very well. Her hairdresser arranged my hair as well, for the occasion. I feel like a princess. This family is such a joy! Ah, Aunt Fearn, if only you could meet the mister. The true measure of a father is his children. The children (and their children) have been arriving all day. Each and every one is overjoyed to greet the father and be greeted. Such unabashed hugging and laughing and even a few happy tears! Tis a jolly season, of course, but the love in this house lifts the season above mere jollity. I had never before imagined how much a good father brings to the warmth of a home.

"Linnet, your young man's come." Marisetta's voice outside her door ended all thoughts of correspondence. Linnet left the ink pot open and bounded for the door. She remembered propriety barely in time. She stopped, took a deep breath, patted her hair. Her head high, she glided out into the hall.

She expected to see a coachman waiting. At the far end there stood James himself, his hat in his hand. He had just accepted a glass of brandy from the tray Marisetta's nephew passed around, and he and Mr. Higgins were both chatting and nodding cheerfully. Mr. Higgins held a huge pudding, obviously a gift. James carried a bulky fur wrap of some sort over his arm.

James glanced her way and froze, dumbstruck, the brandy snifter halfway to his lips. The handsome grin exploded like sunshine across his face. All the spoken compliments in the world could not have said as much as that admiring gaze. A princess? Linnet felt like a queen!

He sipped at his brandy and watched her come. His eyes were doing much the same things Gib's had done at Cumberland House that night so long ago, but it was not the same thing; not at all!

"Mmm!" Mr. Higgins purred. "Y'r glorious, lass. Here you go." He reached for Linnet's wool cape.

James held up a hand. "It's a hideously cold night. Perhaps this will serve better." He snapped his fur wrap open. It was a dark, rich brown, the fur incredibly soft. He draped it across her shoulders.

Linnet ought to say something, but as usual, when she needed words most they utterly failed her. She stammered something polite and muttered a few good evenings. She saw Mrs. Higgins lingering in the parlor doorway. Linnet waved good-by to her.

"Have a fine evening, lass." Mr. Higgins patted her fur-wrapped shoulder. "Take good care of her, Mr. Landry. She's a jewel."

Impulsively Linnet stretched to tiptoe and planted a rapid kiss on Mr. Higgins's cheek. "Thank you, sir! Good evening." That was hardly the way for a maid to treat her employer! She was forgetting her place already! She would apologize for her indiscretion tomorrow. Right now she was much too filled with anticipation and bubbling good cheer.

The carriage, large enough to require two horses, was slung low between its wheels. It was the elegant sort of conveyance Linnet had often seen pass as she walked from here to there. She had never dreamt of riding in one. The coachman in his long black cape watched from the lofty box. The footman gave her a hand up and in. The moment James followed her inside, the footman snatched away the little stepping stool. The door slammed. They were encased in complete blackness. Linnet regretted that the curtains were drawn against the cold. No one could see her riding in the midst of all this splendor.

"You are absolutely stunning tonight, my dear." The leather seat crackled as James pulled her in close. "When I heard you were staying with Hector Higgins I asked around a little—discreetly, of course. Fine reputation the man has. Family friend?"

So he didn't know she was a humble maid. Well, she certainly wasn't going to find out from her. "In a way. You know, I think I like Montreal every bit as much as Detroit. Perhaps even more." She giggled. "I'm so happy you weren't stuck at Cumberland or Fort William. Or even York. You'd be a babbling lunatic by now."

He laughed. "Oh, no, I wouldn't. I'd be slogging

the width of Canada on snowshoes, placing foot before foot and staring straight ahead into the blinding blizzard, gritting my teeth, doggedly determined to escape that forsaken wilderness—to find someplace, anyplace, where they know how to properly prepare lamb and beef. Where they use clean sheets on the beds."

She nodded in the chill darkness. " 'Doggedly determined.' Yes, that's you. You always get what you want eventually, whatever it is."

"Yes, I do eventually." His voice, his face, hovered close to her. His free hand brushed along her shoulder and curled itself around the side of her head. He drew her to himself in another of those exciting, frightening kisses.

She was tense, on guard. She could feel it. Deliberately she forced herself to relax against him. Running was such foolishness. Why did she do it back in that swamp? And why did she have such a terrible urge to escape now? The arm around her shoulders pulled her in tighter. The fingertips of his free hand traced tantalizing little lines up and down her throat.

Soft and tickly, the fingertips drew random little circles around her ears. She suddenly wondered just how far those fingertips intended to go. When she had taken in the bodice and raised the waistline on this gown, she had been careful not to raise the already low neckline. That may have been an error. His touch was so light that

"Mr. Landry!" Her eyes popped open. She grabbed his wrist.

He pulled his wrist toward himself. The warm, moist lips kissed her knuckles. His voice was firm and patient, that of a man explaining something to a child who should already know the explanation. "Linnet, you're not a little schoolgirl fresh from sponging off the slates. You're a mature woman, and it's long past time you began enjoying your maturity." He chuckled and kissed her knuckles again, affectionately. "But you needn't worry about propriety. The ride is too short for anything serious. Besides, neither you nor I would wish to appear at a sophisticated social function in a state of disarray."

She giggled in spite of herself.

"Therefore your modesty is assured—for the moment." His voice grew serious. "But as you yourself point out, I get what I want. And I've come to realize that I've wanted you ever since I first saw you in that dumpy little wool dress at Cumberland. I promise you," his voice dropped to a quiet purr. "this will be the most exciting, most romantic night of your life."

If his other kisses frightened her, she should be terrified of this one. It fused her lips to himself, pressed her to himself, melted her into himself, lifted her away to some sort of floating brightness. She ought to grab his wrist again, but she was suddenly afraid she might displease him; he turned surly so easily and quickly. She did not want in any way to displease him tonight, this night of nights.

The coach lurched to a stop.

Linnet heard the stepping stool rattle against the frozen ground. When the door swung open they were both sitting very primly erect. The coachman helped her down. She stepped into the crunchy snow and pulled the fur close around.

Directly before them the door to a great hall splashed brilliant yellow brightness across the snowy street. It squandered light as if light were not at all a precious commodity in this long winter darkness. Linnet could sense the attraction toward light that every moth feels. The bright doorway beckoned as she climbed the steps on James's sturdy arm.

They stepped inside. Instantly a doorman lifted the cape from Linnet's shoulders. The great hall blazed with light—banks of candles, lamps, chandeliers. Everything sparkled.

Directly across from the door an elaborate white fireplace stretched up through the ceiling. Its hearth yawned so big a man might stand in it. There was another fireplace at the far end, equally elaborate—and another—no wonder the room was warm as summer; tree-sized logs crackled in four giant fireplaces.

Linnet tried not to gape, but she stood in awe a moment. She was floating now in a totally new world. She might as well be in London or Paris amid the very height of society, for every person here reflected the sort of fashion you would see in the biggest cities. Every lady present was dressed in silks and glittering jewelry. Even portly ladies benefitted from the very high waistlines and flattering sashes. Every man present was the picture of elegance in ruffled shirts and slim cutaway jackets.

Linnet had just about absorbed all this glamour when she caught her breath in surprise. One man here had not decked himself out in tight trousers and ruffled finery. He wore his usual country coat. His trousers flapped unfashionably loose around his legs. He looked the same here as he looked at Cumberland House and at Lac Bouleau. Simon McLaren stood beside the vast fireplace chatting with a plump older lady.

James was gaping, too. "Somehow I assumed that he was spending the winter in the back country there." He snorted. "I'm surprised that sober-sided old Calvinist would tarnish his halo by appearing here."

Linnet called her wits back to order. She shouldn't be so surprised; as a ranking officer in a major fur company, Simon might be expected to attend this great social occasion. She glanced up at James. "Aren't you being a bit snide?"

"Sorry." He smiled at her, almost contrite. "I was taken aback. I didn't know he was in the city, and he doesn't seem the sort to fit in here."

"Why, James!" A lady's cultured voice interrupted from beyond James's other elbow. "Here you are." Linnet leaned out and around him to get a look. The young woman appeared stunning in a pale pink gown of some gauzy sort of fabric. Rich coppery-brown curls crowded together at the back of her head and bobbed charmingly whenever she moved.

James stepped back a little. "Linnet, this is Penelope Dawes, daughter of a long-time business friend from London. Pen, Linnet MacLeod."

"How do you do, Miss Dawes." Linnet manufactured a smile.

"An American fresh from the backwoods. How quaint. My pleasure, Miss MacLeod."

James nodded to her. "Have a fine evening with your young man there, Pen. And greet your father for me, please."

"Greet him yourself. He's here tonight." The lady glanced at Linnet. "You'll excuse us a moment, dear? Only a moment. There's a dear."

"Of course . . ." Linnet had no idea what the appropriate response was.

James patted her hand. "I'll be right back. Pen's father and I are old friends." And away he went with those curls bouncing by his shoulder.

Penelope was wagging her lovely head. "Congratulations. You win the bet. I cede. A total stranger in this town and you come up with a companion on two days' notice. You must really be a . . ." and their voices were lost across the room.

Linnet scowled. Obviously she hadn't heard that

177

quite right. No, the cat's claws were out; Linnet had heard about such women.

People by twos and fours crossed before her and beside her. Should she step out of the way? Would James find her again if she did? This high society business seemed so simple until you got down to the details. James was halfway across the hall now, shaking hands with a balding, rotund gentleman. Penelope hung on James's arm, the arm on which Linnet's hand had rested moments ago.

The musicians stepped onto the dais near the main fireplace and took their seats. The violinist sounded *A*. Linnet's heart took a quick little jump. The music would begin now and she must remember all those elaborate dancing steps. She wished she could practice somehow before dancing with James—make all her mistakes at the beginning so as to appear elegant with him.

"Excuse me. Linnet MacLeod?"

She turned.

A healthy, robust man smiled at her. He appeared young, as if his mother might have pressed those elaborate ruffles on his shirt for him. He dipped his head. "John MacTavish at your service, Miss Mac-Leod. Might I have the honor of this dance?"

"Oh, ah . . ." Linnet looked at James. She raised her eyebrows questioningly.

James was looking at her. He obviously understood the unspoken question; he smiled and nodded across the room.

Linnet turned back to Mr. MacTavish. "I would be delighted, sir." Here was the perfect opportunity to review those hasty dancing lessons without making a fool of herself before James. She offered her hand and the young Mr. MacTavish conducted her across the floor to other couples.

Would this be a minuet or one of those quadrilles?

The couples were assembling themselves in sets of four pairs—a quadrille. Linnet must not lose her train of thought now. A quadrille was more complex and mistakes easier to make. Was she the only person so unsure of herself? These other three women appeared so self-confident. She would keep a close eye on them and follow their cues and movements.

As one, the gentlemen bowed to their consorts. As one, the ladies curtsied deeply in response. Linnet's curtsy (perfected by minutes of practice with the instructor and hours before a mirror) was surely as exaggerated and graceful as anyone else's. She studied the parquet flooring momentarily and stood erect again. She gasped.

Mr. MacTavish was walking quickly away. Before her stood Simon McLaren! It was too late to flee. She was surrounded by dancers and the violin bows were bouncing up the scale. It had begun. She promised herself she would not speak to this devious man. She pressed her lips together. At least it would be good dancing practice.

Along with the other gentlemen, Simon raised his right arm, palm forward. Linnet pressed her palm against his. The dancing master had said that a good partner offered a stiff and solid arm; Simon's arm was rock-solid. They rotated around each other in a full circle like two wary tomcats.

The gentlemen raised their left arms. Simon's barely reached his shoulder. When she pressed her palm to his the whole arm gave way. She practically had to hold it up for him.

She broke that promise to herself. "It's still not well, is it."

They circled.

He smiled and lied, "It'll get better as soon as some summer heat bakes into it."

They separated and walked to opposite sides of the set, circled perfect strangers, and returned.

She gave him a false smile because the other ladies were smiling. "I'm surprised a sober-sided old Calvinist would approve of dancing."

"I don't."

"Then why are you here?"

They separated again in a grand right-and-left. Linnet had to forget everything else and concentrate on getting around the circle without destroying the pattern for everyone. They met at the far side.

He took her hands in his to promenade. "To talk to you."

"You have nothing to say that I want to hear." She looked him squarely in the eye.

"I'm hoping you'll change your mind about that. I only reached town here two weeks ago; had trouble finding you. I heard yesterday you'd be attending tonight, and saw the opportunity to talk to you face to face. Young John MacTavish is one of my clerks here in Montreal." He gave her a firm, but gentle push.

She glided out across the floor and exchanged partners with the woman opposite. Simon guided his opposite through her turns, but his eyes never left Linnet. Now they were together again. They stepped back as the side couples played their parts.

"A disastrous thing happened." He spoke rapidly. "Because of your resentment toward your natural father, you have a wrong picture of what a father is like. And because you hate me, you hate my God. You're letting . . ."

"That's so disastrous?"

"It is. Your Heavenly Father if offering you eternal life. But you can't see that because your feelings about me are blinding you. I urge you to put those feelings aside."

They were separating again. Linnet tried to concentrate and she couldn't. She had only to follow the lady in front of her, yet she very nearly messed it all up. They met briefly and went sweeping off into another of those right-and-left figures. She must have done that correctly; she ended up with Simon on the other side of the set.

He took her hands in the promenade. "Instead, consider God's claims about Jesus without thinking about me at all. Just you and He. Please don't let me be a stumbling block to your salvation. It's much too important. God loves you. He wants you to commit yourself to Him through His son Jesus."

"To live a dull and dreary life forever after. I don't. . ." She stopped. "If you don't approve of dancing, how do you know this quadrille? You're an excellent dancer!"

There was that bemused half smile again. "A red-blooded young Scotsman can find all sorts of amusements if he's amoral enough—everything from Indian girls to pleasures of this sort. Even in the New World. Perhaps even more so in the New World. Dull? Never. The glitter of this world loses its sparkle when you compare it with the sparkle of serving God."

"That's the closest to a confession of sin as I've ever heard from you."

He wagged his head. "I have to confess every day that I'm a sinner, saved only by God's good grace. I hope you can say that also one day. Perhaps . . ."

They separated again in another of those elaborate figures. The musicians were playing the final bars.

Simon raised his right hand and again they circled. "Perhaps when you contemplate God's ways on these cold winter days, you'll see the light. I'm content now. I was restless and unfilled then."

She smiled grimly. "So you think I sin."

"We all do, in thought if not in deed. Any sin hurts the Father deeply."

They circled left. She bit her lip, remembering all those sinful thoughts she had been entertaining lately about James. Sinful? Absolutely. And tonight in the carriage he had as much as promised sin in deed as well as in thought. James. She'd forgotten him until just now.

She curtsied. "I still don't understand. Is this all you wanted to say to me?"

"Yes."

"But . . . ah . . . why did you go to such elaborate lengths—I mean, John MacTavish and everything—to tell me this? Only this?"

"Because it's so important." He bowed without releasing her hand. He kissed her knuckles gently, firmly—warm soft lips pressed against her cool skin.

"Why do you care what I believe?"

"Because I love you so very much."

The music ended.

He was looking at her; his eyes wouldn't turn away. She yanked her hand away and pressed it to her bodice. Others lingered to exchange pleasantries with their dancing partners. Frightened suddenly, for no reason, Linnet wheeled and fled.

She was running. She was darting. She slipped between and around the clusters of gaily chatting fashion plates. The plates stared at her.

James caught her, literally, and swept her aside, away from the crush of people. "By the time I saw what he was pulling it was too late to do anything about it. What a shabby trick! I feel like punching the wily old wolf—forcing himself on you like that."

"No!" She adjusted her voice downward several notches and took a deep breath. "No. He meant well, he really did. He just . . ."

"You look ready to burst into tears." James studied her face. "Come on. We're going out into the dining hall. Give you a chance to pull yourself back together."

He led her quickly around the periphery of the action. They pushed through vast carved doors into another hall—a smaller, narrower one. This hall, lined with long, long tables, was darker than the main hall and much cooler. A few other couples were in here also, standing about in the murky corners of the room. At least two were embracing.

Linnet could hear the orchestra tuning up again. The dancers would be aligning themselves out on the floor. She had no desire ever to perform another minuet or quadrille or galop or any such thing. James came here to dance, so she would surely have to. But the magic was gone.

How could Simon utterly spoil such a lovely evening?

CHAPTER 14

Montreal, at the great ball,
December 24, 1818

Dear God,

I am thinking this letter to You, Divine Father, because I have no means to write. And if I could write it, how would I mail it? As You can see I am sitting here in this cold dining room in the quiet, the only solitary soul in a nest of snuggling couples it seems. As You also know, I asked James to leave me here alone a few minutes to compose myself. What I really must do is think.

I am totally, completely, utterly, absolutely at tag ends. Confused. Frustrated. James has made quite clear what he wants. He seemed very happy to leave me here surrounded by couples who are nuzzling and kissing—the power of suggestion, as it were. And what he wants, I want also. It frightens me, I suppose, to realize I'm just like other women, after all. I am twenty-two years old and I have never let another human being get close enough to matter—

not even Aunt Fearn. That little taste of closeness James has given me convinces me that I want much more. Yet I know that intimacy without marriage is firmly against Your will. O God, what am I to do? As You well know (for I have heard that You search the innermost heart) Your will didn't mean a thing to me before. I can't understand why it does now. Why am I so concerned about what You want when I don't even know You? Why is my conscience such a bother all of a sudden? You are so very real to Simon. I wish You were as real to me. Do You remember when I was talking to my father for that last horrible time and I said I had a father-shaped hole? I'm beginning to think that no earthly father can ever fill it. Does that mean that only You fit it? I know You aren't at all like my father Innis. But are You like Mr. Higgins? And why did Simon have to say he loves me?

Linnet drew a deep, deep breath and squared her shoulders. She must return to James, to the ball, to reality. She must put the confusion aside for now. She walked through the doors out into the great hall. The minuet was just ending. Her eyes scanned the cloud of silks and ruffles along the walls. Surely James would be standing around somewhere on the edge of things; the minuet was already starting when he left. No, there he was, half a head taller than anyone else near him, coming off the floor with Penelope. He had wasted no time in securing a dancing partner! James had never been in the New World before this present journey. Were this Penelope and her father—an "old business friend"—newly met? Or were they Londoners in Montreal temporarily, as was he? The point didn't matter much. Penelope was certainly taking full advantage.

Now that Linnet was back in the brightness and glitter, she shed some of that miserable confusion.

James made a good point; she was a mature woman and it was high time she began to think and act like one. She was here with James; she was here to dance and enjoy the evening. First things first.

Linnet wound amongst the crush of bodies toward James. Penelope might be trying, but James was Linnet's escort and she would claim him. She regretted separating herself from him this long. She had as much as opened the door to Penelope and invited the woman in. Now she must kick the wily conniver out. Brave words! In truth, unfortunately, Linnet did not belong in this group. Uncertain, uncomfortable, unsure of herself, she felt out of place (curious, though: she never had this intense an out-of-place feeling at Cumberland House and beyond). She put the feeling aside, tucked into a dark corner with the confusion. She was an adult, for pity's sake. She could match Penelope any day she cared to.

Linnet pasted a bright smile on her face and glided up to James.

James smiled just as brightly. "There you are!" He turned to Penelope. "I enjoyed the dance immensely. Thank you." He bowed a courtly bow and kissed her hand.

She purred something in response—Linnet couldn't catch her words—and floated off across the room toward the main fireplace.

James gave Linnet's shoulders another of those affectionate squeezes. "Linnet, I admire the way you can deliberately adjust your mood. I wish I could be as much in control of my feelings. It's a rare good trait in a woman. In anyone. You look much cheerier. Do you feel all right now?"

"Quite so," she lied. "You seem to be enjoying yourself here tonight. I'm glad."

He took her hand. Together they wandered off toward refreshment tables at the far end. "I think a part of my enjoyment is simply finding such a high level of civilization. I always looked on this hemisphere as a wasteland of trees and savages and nothing more—and that included the Americans. This is such a surprise and delight.'' He waved an arm and laughed. ''You might say I pictured a whole continent full of Mugwilas.''

Linnet laughed. ''Actually, you know, you could do much worse than Mugwila. Oh, I realize she throws copper pots at you on occasion, and that's not exactly the height of sophistication. But she's a noble woman in the basic sense, the truest sense. And so remarkably capable. There is much to admire in Mugwila.''

''Much indeed, if you fancy cantankerousness. I do not admire independence in a woman. A woman has her place and Mugwila refuses to take that place. I certainly hope you don't look upon her as a paragon to emulate.''

Why should that irritate her? She dismissed the irritation as a product of her own inner turmoil. She was not about to start an argument with James over a woman a thousand miles away or more. She ought to smooth the waters. ''I guess I look on Mugwila as a caring woman who doesn't know how to express her care.'' She giggled suddenly. ''I wouldn't be a bit surprised if Wooly doesn't come knocking at her door the moment he gets back to Cumberland House. He may be there already.''

James chuckled, ''He'll address her as 'ye old bat' when she opens the door. Then he'll give her some sort of gift . . .''

''Oh, yes. Perhaps a shiny new copper kettle he just happened to trade into, or a big hank of beads.''

''Or perhaps some intensely romantic gift like two yards of rawhide or a bucket of bear grease.''

Linnet was smiling, not in ridicule, but in admiration. ''And he'll insist the gift is because of her service to Simon and me, and that he himself still despises her from head to toe."

"And she will speak similar words of love and endearment. Ah, the subtleties of courtship." James wagged his head. That errant curl dropped down. "The reprobate savages are both alike. They deserve each other."

Linnet bit her lip to prevent herself from arguing angrily. She thought the world of Mugwila and Wooly both, but it would serve no purpose to say so now. Neither of them was cultured in the European sense, even though Wooly was probably born a European. Yet each of them willingly suffered discomfort and inconvenience and adversity in order to help others. She thought of Mugwila's gift of painstakingly hand-made moccasins—such a lovely expression of thoughtfulness. She thought of Wooly's deep concern for Simon and his gentle ministrations. Externally they might be rough-cut, but their hearts were genuine. And if Linnet must choose between the likes of Mugwila and the likes of that Penelope Dawes, she'd choose Mugwila every time! She felt a bit as though she were betraying them by not speaking up.

"Here you go." James broke into her thought-world so abruptly she jumped. He placed a delicate punch cup in her hand. "I tried some of this during that first quadrille. Very good stuff."

Linnet could smell the alcohol in it even without raising the cup.

He pressed his hand against the small of her back and piloted her to a quiet corner. By the time they got there his punch glass was nearly empty.

She frowned at his glass. "How much of that have you had, anyway?"

He looked puzzled. "We just got here; what do you mean?"

"I mean all day."

"A little wine with lunch, some brandy following dinner. . . . That reminds me. I was talking to Penelope's father about the shipping seasons. I can be on my way to London fairly early next spring. Montreal opens up long before the Bay."

"I'll regret seeing you go." She really meant it, too. So he had either lunch or dinner with Penelope and her father.

He backed her into the corner and stood very close. His hovering, manly bulk sealed off the world, insulated her from its bustle and glitter. It was only the two of them here now. "I don't want you to see me go. I want you to come with me."

"To London? *Me?* But . . ."

"Why not you? Frankly speaking, you're much too nice for Detroit. You're too pretty, too clever, too smart to waste yourself on that backwoods village."

"I'd hardly call it a village. Of course it's not half the town Montreal is, but . . ."

"A village. Oh, I suppose London will take some getting used to if you've spent your whole life in the woods. But I'm sure you'll love the place. There's a feel about it—you know you're at the hub of the world. And I don't want to leave you behind. I want to enjoy you every moment. I want to be the one to teach you the arts of love."

Her mouth dropped open. She closed it quickly. "James, is this a marriage proposal?"

His voice took on that glassy smoothness she heard when he told Gib everything was all right—and it wasn't. "Montreal may pass for culture, but marry here? Hardly. That would be like conducting a high mass in a horse paddock. No, I'll marry in London when I marry, with all the pomp and trimmings. St. Paul's, St. John's perhaps. I'm certain you'll agree with me, once you see the place."

"I think I see quite a bit right now. And until the ship sails?"

His finger traced a tantalizing trail from shoulder to shoulder along the neckline of her dress. "Take each day as it comes. The house where I'm staying is quite spacious. Oh, there are a few bearskin rugs on the floors, but all in all it's quite up to Old World standards. I hope you realize how welcome you would be, if you choose. I can assure you it will be an exciting winter, a romantic winter. Surely you don't want to spend all those long nights hibernating when there's so much to do—parties, balls, dinners. I'm certain the Higginses are lovely people, but I should think life in their home is more than a bit on the slow side. For example, they aren't here tonight."

She thought about the Higginses at home. No, they weren't here tonight. They were at home with the children who loved them so much, and their grandchildren. They were laughing and talking and enjoying Marisetta's superb cooking. They were basking in warmth and closeness. And joy. Real, genuine, heartfilling joy. Not empty glitter.

"Dull evenings or bright gaiety," he purred. "Not such a hard choice, I should think. And thrilling new sensations you've never dreamt of."

"Isn't it strange? If you had suggested all this a month ago I probably would have accepted on the spot. But . . . well, ah . . . I think I must have changed. Become more wary, perhaps. And I don't know why, but I have. I don't think I can. No, I know I can't. You're a magnificent man, a charming man. I was quite taken with you the first time I saw you. I'll marry you this very moment if you ask me. But without marriage? No. Not in London, not before London. Not tonight." She whispered, "I'm sorry."

He studied her face a long moment. "Did I say take each day as it comes? Let's make it each hour as it comes. This next hour shall be devoted to dancing. They're assembling on the floor now. Drink your punch and let's join them."

"I . . . I'd rather not drink this. Thank you anyway. It's much too strong for me. Too much rum."

"Blast, Linnet! Grow up!" He stepped back. "What's the matter with you, anyway? When we arrived you were ready for anything. All smiles."

"Simon said he loves me!" she blurted. She gasped; the thought had not even crossed her mind until her lips spoke the words.

He stared at her. "What in the name of John has that to do with anything? McLaren is a meddling old fool. He doesn't belong here and he doesn't belong in your life. Forget whatever it is he told you. Just remember the sneaky way he managed to reach you. Now let's . . ."

"He was taking his Father's part. He didn't . . ."

"Fathers? If you choose to play the part of the child—a child in a woman's lovely body, I might add—then I shall play father, if that's what you want. Drink up now, little girl, with no further ado, and we'll join the dance. Come along."

"With another cup of punch to follow, and another, until I'm flexible enough to do whatever you wish. That's not the part of a father, James."

"You're hardly the one to tell me what a father is like!" He clamped his mouth down to a thin white line and inhaled. "This argument has gone much too far already. I've been pushing too hard—an error on my part. I apologize. So I shall back off. I'm sorry I came on so strongly. Of course, you should do whatever feels right to you. Relax. Sip your drink there. Let's both cool off and start over in a few minutes." He smiled suddenly. "They say opposites attract, and that true love never runs smooth." He chuckled. "We certainly aren't running smooth just now, are we? I'll

191

be back shortly." He gave her a brotherly peck on the forehead and squeezed her shoulders again.

"Unless your intentions are simply to enjoy the dancing and nothing more, don't bother."

"Now you really are acting like Mugwila. But she had her own canoe. It's my fur wrap and my carriage. As I said, I'll be back shortly." He walked off. His look of smug supremacy infuriated her, probably because he was right. Linnet closed her eyes. They burned. Simon caused all this. It was his fault. She opened them again. No, it wasn't. Of course, it wasn't. He was as honest and principled as James was devious. Linnet certainly wasn't going to be dancing this next set, but she knew what she was going to do. She should have done it a long, long time ago. She walked out into the hall, side-stepping faceless couples. There was a servant over there; he was an older man and perhaps, therefore, the major-domo. She crossed to him.

"Excuse me. Do you know a man named Simon McLaren when you see him?"

"Yes, Madame."

"Where is he now? Has he left?"

"I don't believe so, Madame. You might look for him in the blue room."

"The blue room."

"Through there, Madame." The man pointed to a ceiling-high set of mahogany doors.

"Thank you." She crossed back around the hollow, glittering hall, past two crackling fireplaces. The ornate doors, huge as a fortress gate, stood slightly ajar. Linnet slipped in through them soundlessly.

On the far side of the narrow room, a poorly tended fire struggled to stay alive in another of those gargantuan fireplaces. He sat alone, encased in a wingback chair with his left side toward her. His elbows flopped listlessly on the chair's arms; his legs

192

sprawled at odd angles. The orange glow from the fireplace made his face appear older and craggier than she knew it to be. She stood there awhile, simply watching him. She yearned for his encircling hug. He looked so . . . so . . . so complete. He didn't need her. He didn't need anybody.

She needed him.

He might be in the thick of civilization, but his woodland instincts still prevailed. Like the wild animals who can sense being watched, he detected her though she made no sound or movement. He turned his head toward her.

She took a few steps and dreaded moving closer. She stopped. 'You're not dancing.''

He stood up. ''Neither are you.''

''I, ah . . .'' She couldn't talk from this far away. She closed the distance and stood before him. ''I came to, ah . . . ask your . . . to apologize for the way I've acted toward you these last several months. I ask your forgiveness.'' She studied the thick braided rug at their feet.

His warm hand tipped her chin up. He looked her squarely in the eyes. ''You are freely forgiven.''

''Th–thank you.'' She twisted her face away in order to examine the rug in greater detail. She must not say much more. She was too close to tears now. ''I hope you enjoy the evening. And Merry Christmas. Good night.'' She turned away toward the distant doors.

''I assume you're returning to James.'' He sounded sad, disappointed.

She stopped. ''No. No, I'm not. We're going our separate ways. We, ah, failed to see eye to eye on certain issues.''

''Shall I take you home?''

''Thank you, but you should return to your companion.''

"I'm unaccompanied. I was about to leave anyway."

She turned to him. "Those few moments you stole out there on the dance floor—I really am the only reason you came tonight."

He smiled, but the smile lacked its bemused twinkle. He extended his arm and she laid her hand on it; it was exactly the same gesture as when first they met those long, long days ago. They walked in silence through the towering doors. They crossed the corner of the ballroom on their way to the entrance foyer.

A minuet was in progress—somewhere around the first third of it, if Linnet remembered her lessons rightly. She searched for him quickly; there was James, fir-tree tall, near the center. He was dancing with Penelope again. Wasn't Penelope escorted here tonight? Yes. Her father stood by the big fireplace and a greatly irritated young man at his elbow was scowling and talking a mile a minute. The fellow looked and acted like a discarded escort. And Penelope's father was nodding and smiling and watching his daughter and not hearing a word of the torrent by his ear.

James noticed her just as she and Simon were about to disappear into the foyer. She hesitated, hoping jealousy would overcome his lust. She hoped he would come running to pledge his love, to agree to a moral union, to . . .

He stopped cold in the middle of a rosette. The man behind bumped into him. James stared at her for long moments. Suddenly he turned away and was swept back into the figure.

The major-domo handed Simon his coat, a long blanket capote. The man's assistant at the door started to lay that fur cape over Linnet's shoulders.

"No." She held up her hand. "Give the cape to Mr. James Landry, please, on his way out. It's his."

The assistant looked at her blankly, but Simon caught on instantly. Without a word he draped his blanket capote around her. She was amazed how heavy it was. He smiled and addressed the major-domo by name—she didn't discern what he said. Suddenly they were outside in the bitter cold. The snow was falling again. Huge heavy flakes swirled and shoved, fighting to be the first down to cover the ground. As they reached streetside, a closed carriage came rattling to the curb. Looking frightfully cold, a small boy held the door open. Simon gave her a firm right hand up and in. He told the coachman her address and hopped in beside her. The door slammed.

She settled onto the crackly-cold leather seat and pulled the capote closer around. "How did your carriage know you were leaving now?"

"Larson sent the boy out ahead when he saw us coming. Remarkably efficient man, Larson."

Remarkably. *Just like you, Simon McLaren. So efficient, so self-sufficient, you don't seem to need anyone, not even when you're lying helpless in a ruined cabin on Lac Bouleau.*

They rode in silence made all the more deafening by the racket of iron wheels on the frozen ruts. They were alone in this carriage, the only two people in the world. The windows were frosted opaque. James had stolen an ardent kiss because it was expected of a man in this situation. Simon just sat there. Could it be that what James said about Simon was true? Well, it was none of Linnet's business, or James's either for that matter, whether it were true or not. It didn't matter anyway.

Her voice spoke unprompted by her mind. "A source who will remain nameless couldn't believe that you, ah, failed to approach me when we were alone all that time at Lac Bouleau. The source feels that perhaps, ah, your manhood has abated."

He sniffed, a bitter little snicker. "To the immoral, self-control may well appear to be impotence. It's self-control, all the same."

"How did your wife die?" Her question startled her. She shouldn't ask.

"Exposure. She died of cold."

"Rumor at Cumberland House was that you killed her."

"In a way I did." His voice riffled like a stream-water across shallow stones. "She was half Cree and half Scots—what they call in this country a native. A round, jolly girl, dry sense of humor, excellent cook, a very pleasant companion. My friends—Wooly among them—warned me against marrying, but of course I knew best. I thought that if she wore different clothes and lived in a different house, she'd fit in here. After all, she was half European by blood already."

"Most men marry natives, I understand."

"And stay in the woods. I bought her fancy European clothes and built her a fine big house here in Montreal. I took her to London with me last spring. There wasn't a day there that she didn't shed tears. Last summer, I took her along to Fort William and Cumberland. She seemed happier. Until August. Middle of August I flipped a canoe and she was swept down through a rocky cascade."

"That explains it! What Wooly said to you when we took what he called a sleigh ride. You lost your wife in a canoeing accident."

"She didn't die. Not just then. But she miscarried, probably at about five months along. It would have been a boy. She never quite recovered. I brought her back here, thinking that a quiet winter in a warm house would mend her. The twinkle in her eye went first. She got weaker. I'd go out for the day and return to find her in the same position as when I left.

"One night in February the weather snapped

especially cold. We both commented on it. Our intimacy that night was more enthusiastic, more passionate, than it had been for months. I thought she had turned around and was starting to get better. When I awoke in the morning she was gone. She had risen during the night and simply walked out into the streets, unclad. Sometime during the night she . . ." his voice cracked, "she fell asleep. They found her two miles from the house."

Linnet thought about that feverish old woman who had deliberately wandered away from the Métis camp. Her heart ached.

Simon continued, "The fact that she was an agent's wife, or that she wore lovely clothes, didn't make any difference. She was rejected socially—snubbed when I escorted her, uninvited to ladies' affairs. There was no place for her, and I was the one who brought her here. If I'd left her in the woods . . . I spent enough winters in a wigwam to know they're just as comfortable as a fancy house. Yes," he sighed, "the rumor at Cumberland is true."

Tears traced hot trails down her chilled cheeks, but the tears were not for herself this time. "Didn't God forgive you for all that?"

"Yes. But I couldn't forgive myself, until Wooly reminded me of God's sovereignty."

"Did she come east of her own choice, or did you make her?"

"She wanted to come. But she didn't realize . . ."

"Didn't she ask you to take her back home to the woods?"

"No, but I should have seen . . ."

"Then if you must shoulder the blame for her death, at least let her carry the greater part of the burden. She made a wrong choice, unfair to you and disastrous to herself. But it was *her* choice."

"You don't understand. The husband is the head of

the household, responsible for its members. I should have seen how sick she was. I should have . . ."

"No!" Linnet snapped. "She had a responsibility to you, too, to tell you her true feelings. She should have told you. She should never have gone and—and done *that*. She should have . . ."

"Stop it! She did what she did because she . . ." He took a deep breath. "I'm sorry. Apparently it hasn't been long enough yet since she . . ." His voice dribbled away to nothing.

"I want to get out of here, please. I just want to walk awhile. Too much is happening too quickly. I need—I want . . ." She scooted forward to the edge of the seat.

He reached up and rapped on the roof. They lurched to a halt. "I'll accompany you."

"No. I'll go alone, please. Thank you anyway. Oh. Your coat here . . ."

The carriage door opened. Somewhere out in the blackness stood the waiting coachman.

"I'll call for it later. Are you sure you want to . . . ?"

"I'm sure." She hopped down into the snow, into the darkness. She began to walk briskly, for the air, icy cold, pinched her face. It seemed every parlor was lighted tonight, and every home merry. The light from the windows turned most of the street a mellow gold.

Linnet had expected that somehow this walk would clear her muddled thoughts. It did no such thing. The more she tried to sift through all that had happened tonight, the murkier her thoughts became. One clear thought was James. He was exactly the sort of man Aunt Fearn had warned her about. How could she have been so blinded to his lecherous intentions, his selfishness, his arrogance? That beautiful face and wavy hair hid such rottenness.

And Simon—poor Simon. He was right. February,

ten months ago, was much too soon for his wounds to heal. She should never have said what she said about the dear wife he obviously loved so much. She remembered now what Wooly had said to Mugwila. "He married your kind, and he loved her." Why did her erring mouth always say things that should not be said?

Her erring mouth grievously wounded her father, too. She should not have said those things either. The bitterness in her heart made her eyes burn. She sniffled, too full of regret to appreciate the cheer of this festive Eve. Yet she must put on a happier face, for there was the Higgins parlor window just ahead.

The candlelight came pouring out, the brightest window on the block. She could barely hear the chatter and laughter inside.

A shadow moved near the front door. Linnet gasped. Should she step closer into the street? Was it danger?

"Linnet, lass." A husky voice whispered from the blackness between.

"Who . . . ?" Linnet glanced around quickly. A carriage paused along the curb in the dim darkness half a block beyond. Simon! He had been watching her, making certain she returned safely home. Simon felt the responsibility to protect her even when she rejected him! Would James have done that? Hah! But the carriage was pulling away now, dissolved in blackness. Now, when she needed Simon most . . .

"Linnet." The figure stepped out into the half light of the parlor window.

"Oooh." Her knees melted and she plopped into the skiff of new snow, her hands clasped over her mouth. Her flittering mind had now betrayed her completely; she was seeing ghosts, fantasies from her tortured soul.

Innis MacLeod dropped to his knees in front of her.

Hesitantly, his hand reached out and gently touched her cheek. The finger was warm. Ghosts are not warm. Neither do they lift you carefully to your feet in strong arms.

Linnet shook her head, incredulous. Finally she managed to find her tongue. "Come. Over here." She tugged at him, drawing him closer to the window. She peered into those eyes that were her own eyes. She cupped her hands around that bushy face. "It *is* you. How did . . . ? I don't understand . . ." The enormity of it all engulfed her. She threw her arms around his neck and clung, sobbing. Those brawny arms as strong as Simon's pressed her close.

"I didn't—I couldn't—I felt so bad," she stammered. She sucked in a deep breath and started over. "I treated you so badly. I was wrong. You said you did the best you could for us. That's the most any father can do. And I couldn't accept—the fault was mine but I blamed you, and . . . and . . ." She shuddered. "I wanted so much to make amends—to ask your forgiveness—but I thought you were gone." She loosened her embrace and pulled back enough to see into his face. "How did you survive?"

His teeth shone yellow in the dim light. "Wouldn't have. But Simon came back for me."

"Simon!" Her arms fell loose. "That's where he went; he left us at Fort William and went—went back. But we were days getting out."

He wagged his head. "No one was more surprised than I, when I woke up at the bottom of that gorge and not in hell or heaven. I managed to find shelter, built a bough bed. Your party left pemmican behind—on purpose, now I see. Took Simon eleven days to return, he said, though I lost count. Took us near another two weeks to raise Fort William and 'til just a week ago to reach Montreal. I would'a died without him, lass."

Linnet's head was reeling too fast to hold thoughts. "How did he know you had survived?"

"He didn't. Just came back to sweep up what was left. Didn't want to recover the body with that Bay man waiting to snatch it for a prize. Didn't want to spend time looking for me and maybe get you trapped by snow. Felt his first duty was to you." Innis MacLeod had aged a decade in these last few months. His lips trembled. "Responsibility, lass. I see now I failed it, drafts be naught. Simon, he's always been that way—keen on responsibility. Myself? I've never had a dollop of the stuff. I ask ye to forgive me for neglecting your dear Mum and you. Ye know I always loved you both."

"And I ask you to forgive me for my hatred and bitterness. I wronged you, too." Linnet realized as she spoke them that she meant those words; her heart was echoing them.

Her father gripped both her shoulders and pushed her back a bit, the better to study her face. "Listen carefully, lass. I'm a marked man, a wanted man and rightly so. What they accuse me of is true and more. Until tonight I was staying at Simon's house. Now I'm . . ."

"I talked to him moments ago. Why didn't he mention you?"

"Eh, I asked him not to. Besides, he felt that ye despise me so much I could do no good by coming back into your life. I had in mind just to get one last good look at ye before I went away. But then I heard myself speaking your name."

"Where are you going?"

The life-worn face cracked into a mirthless smile. "This old trapper's still not a man of responsibility, lass—not the one to quietly give myself up. They're out to get me, aye, but they'll have to work some to do it. I've left Simon's roof but Simon knows not where I be, and ye shan't, and even I don't. Likely, I won't survive the winter. I'm too stove up and old. So I'm off to somewhere, it matters not where. And yourself, lass—ye must get on with your own life." He purred, "Ah, ye be a braw young lady, Linnet. A source of great pride to me. Go now." He patted her shoulders. He murmured it again, "Go now," and stepped back into the shadows between the buildings. As the ghost had come, now he left, disappearing into the blackness.

"Wait!" She took a step forward and caught herself. He was gone, and in the way he wanted. Somehow, it was what she wanted, too. Yet . . .

Her heart overflowed and bubbled up into pouring tears. They coursed down her cheeks in riffling streams.

Simon. She knew what she must do now. The confusion was clearing and one bright, stark thought emerged. She began to run through the slippery new snow, past the Higginses' door into the darkness upstreet. She jogged out into the street, the better to follow the fresh carriage tracks. Already the big puffy flakes were starting to obscure them.

Simon! Never in all the months she had known him had Simon ever insisted on his own wishes, nor had he fought for what he himself wanted. Always he tried so hard to protect her. He protected her physically, putting himself between her and danger. Right or wrong he even tried to protect her from the truth about her father. He even protected her from Gib. And she wore his blanket capote now.

He said he loved her very much. Only just now did she realize that his kiss was no mere stratagem to fool Gib. And tonight he spent those few precious moments on the dance floor pleading not his own case but God's.

She stopped so quickly she slipped in the loose

202

snow and fell. Boot prints appeared beside the wheel marks. Simon had left his carriage. Perhaps like she, he preferred to walk, for there were no fine houses near. He could not be home here. The wheelmarks disappeared around the corner. She followed the footprints up the dark street.

In the dead of night, falling snow generates a certain grayness—almost light, but not quite. It filled the air around her. Her eyes burned.

This was foolish! She could never find him in this darkness; she could never catch up to him. She would never—there he was! The black coat loomed in the vague and momentary light of a window two blocks ahead. It melted instantly into blackness. She broke into a clumsy run. Her soft slippers slid about in the loose, dry snow. Her toes ached.

"Simon! Simon, wait!" Surely the whole city heard her!

She could make him out again, just barely, black against black. He wheeled around.

The frozen air burned her lungs and tightened her throat. She could not breathe; she could not speak as she caught up to him. She slipped when she stopped in front of him; he grabbed her to keep her from falling.

"I was . . ." She swallowed and inhaled. "I was . . . afraid . . ." The cold air stabbed inside her breast. She could see his face clearly now in the cold gray snow-glow. "I was afraid . . . I couldn't catch up to you."

The corners of his mouth tilted upward into a grim little false smile. "I walk a couple yards and have to stop and wipe my glasses off. They keep fogging up." His cheeks were wet, too.

"You said you love me. Do you love me?" Air came in great gulps.

"Yes! Yes, I love you."

"I speak out, too . . ." She stopped and started

over. "I speak out when I mustn't, and I do things I shouldn't, and when I want to do something right, it keeps coming out wrong, and I'm not nearly as good as I should be or want to be, but . . ." She was still breathless, but not from running. She hung her whole life out like clothes on a line, all suspended from one foolish impertinent question. "But will you have me anyway?"

She waited for an answer. He made none. For centuries he studied her eyes. His glasses started to fog over again. His lips moved to frame a reply, but nothing came out. Suddenly, without warning, he engulfed her in a massive squeeze. His chest heaved outward in a deep breath, tightening the hug even more. His hand pressed her head against his cheek and shoulder.

She crushed herself in still closer. "I'm so foolish about men." She was losing her composure—what little was left of it. "I didn't realize I needed you until you walked away. I mean, I really needed you. I didn't know myself. What I . . . I mean . . ." She heaved a shuddering sigh. She had run out of words again.

Apparently so had he. His warm, gentle hand tipped her face up. His warm, gentle lips set her floating again, and it was no stratagem this time. No shallow glitter, no false promise, no casual and temporary passion lurked beneath this kiss. It was real. Simon was real. Her quest was ended.

MEET THE AUTHOR

SANDY DENGLER, the desert rat, replete with degree in Desert Ecology, married a lemming—a man in love with the Far North. Her husband's subscription to the Hudson's Bay Company in-house magazine sparked her own interest in the fur country and the fur-trade rivalries of the early nineteenth century.

Besides all those years of Hudson's Bay Company *Beaver* back issues, her husband now owns a classic wood-canvas Old Town canoe; Sandy now knows which end of a canoe paddle to put in the water. They've toted the canoe from Maine to California to Washington State, where he has worked in the national parks as a ranger.

The Denglers have brought up two daughters—one, a high school senior; the other, a university biology major. The girls' most vivid memory of canoeing is the constant harsh admonition: "Sit still and quit trailing your fingers in the water!"

Serenade/Saga Books are inspirational romances in historical settings, designed to bring you a joyful, heart-lifting reading experience.

Other Serenade/Saga books available in your local bookstore:

Watch for these Serenade Books in the months to come:

A Letter To Our Readers

Dear Reader:

Pioneering is an exhilarating experience, filled with opportunities for exploring new frontiers. The Zondervan Corporation is proud to be the first major publisher to launch a series of inspirational romances designed to inspire and uplift as well as to provide wholesome entertainment. In order that we might better contribute to your reading enjoyment, we would appreciate your taking a few minutes to respond to the following questions and return to:

> Anne Severance, Editor
> Serenade/Saga Books
> 1415 Lake Drive, S.E.
> Grand Rapids, Michigan 49506

1. Did you enjoy reading WINTERSPRING?

   ☐ Very much. I would like to see more books by this author!

   ☐ Moderately

   ☐ I would have enjoyed it more if _____

2. Where did you purchase this book? _____

3. What influenced your decision to purchase this book?

   ☐ Cover   ☐ Back cover copy
   ☐ Title   ☐ Friends
   ☐ Publicity   ☐ Other _____

4. Please rate the following elements from 1 (poor) to 10 (superior):

☐ Heroine   ☐ Plot
☐ Hero   ☐ Inspirational theme
☐ Setting   ☐ Secondary characters

5. Which settings would you like to see in future Serenade/Saga Books?

_____   _____

_____   _____

6. What are some inspirational themes you would like to see treated in Serenade books?

_____   _____

_____   _____

7. Would you be interested in reading other Serenade/Serenata or Serenade/Saga Books?

☐ Very interested
☐ Moderately interested
☐ Not interested

8. Please indicate your age range:

☐ Under 18   ☐ 25–34   ☐ 46–55
☐ 18–24   ☐ 35–45   ☐ Over 55

9. Would you be interested in a Serenade book club? If so, please give us your name and address:

Name _____

Occupation _____

Address _____

City _____ State _____ Zip _____